Other Books by Janet Tashjian

• *My Life as a Book*
• *Fault Line*
• *Multiple Choice*
• *Tru Confessions*
• *Marty Frye, Private Eye*

The Larry Series:
• *The Gospel According to Larry*
• *Vote for Larry*
• *Larry and the Meaning of Life*

My Life
as a
Stuntboy

Praise for

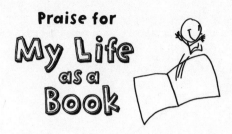

My Life as a Book

☆ "Dryly hilarious first-person voice. . . . A kinder, gentler Wimpy Kid with all the fun and more plot."
—*Kirkus Reviews*, starred review

☆ "Janet Tashjian, known for her young adult books, offers a novel that's part *Diary of a Wimpy Kid*, part intriguing mystery. . . . Give this to kids who think they don't like reading. It might change their minds."
—*Booklist*, starred review

"Derek is a smooth narrator with a strong, humorous voice. . . . Derek tells readers, 'If my life were a book, I'd have my own cool adventures.' It is, and he does."
—*The Horn Book*

"The protagonist is by turns likable and irritating, but always interesting. He is sure to engage fans of Jeff Kinney's *Diary of a Wimpy Kid* books as well as those looking for a spunky, contemporary boy with a mystery to solve."
—*School Library Journal*

"Tashjian forgoes the lecture on the importance of reading and instead allows Derek's summer to unfold organically, implicitly highlighting the various learning experiences kids have outside of formal education. . . . Comparisons to Kinney's *Wimpy Kid* are no doubt likely, and this will particularly gratify the younger end of that fan base."
—*BCCB*

JANET TASHJIAN

My Life as a Stuntboy

with cartoons by
JAKE TASHJIAN

Christy Ottaviano Books
Henry Holt and Company
New York

Henry Holt and Company, LLC
Publishers since 1866
175 Fifth Avenue
New York, New York 10010
mackids.com

Henry Holt® is a registered trademark of
Henry Holt and Company, LLC.

Library of Congress Cataloging-in-Publication Data
Tashjian, Janet.
My life as a stuntboy / Janet Tashjian ; with cartoons by
Jake Tashjian. — 1st ed.
     p.   cm.
"Christy Ottaviano Books."
Summary: Twelve-year-old Derek Fallon has the
opportunity of a lifetime—to perform stunts in a movie
featuring a popular twelve-year-old star—but
complications arise involving his best friend, a capuchin
monkey, and Derek's chronic inability to concentrate on
schoolwork.
ISBN 978-0-8050-8904-2
[1. Stunt performers—Fiction. 2. Motion pictures—
Production and direction—Fiction. 3. Monkeys as
pets—Fiction. 4. Schools—Fiction. 5. Family life—
California—Los Angeles—Fiction. 6. Los Angeles
(Calif.)—Fiction. 7. Children's art.] I. Tashjian, Jake, ill.
II. Title.
PZ7.T211135Myf 2011
[Fic]—dc22

                                              2010029884

First edition—2011
Book design by Elynn Cohen

Printed in the United States of America by
LSC Communications, Harrisonburg, Virginia.

20 19 18 17 16 15 14 13 12

For Doug

My Life
as a
Stuntboy

Help!

THE FIRST DAY OF SCHOOL IS always the worst day of the year. It's like some crazy surgeon throws you on an operating table and removes a major organ from your chest called summer. He doesn't realize how much a kid *needs* that organ, as much as a liver or a spleen.

surgeon

I feel almost bruised being back at school, and I haven't even made it

bruised

to class yet. Maybe if I go to the nurse, she'll take pity on me and hook me up to an emergency life support system. But before I can make any last wishes, my friend Matt punches me in the arm and jolts me back from my daytime nightmare.

"This year definitely won't be as bad as the others." Matt realizes the price tag is hanging from the sleeve of his shirt so he yanks it off as we talk.

When we found out we would have Mr. Maroni this year, Matt and I were *almost* excited about school.

"It'll be great to finally have a guy teacher—I've never had one." I imagine a school filled with male teachers, couches, potato chips, and flat-screen TVs.

Matt shakes me from my reverie

reverie

by making a buzzing noise like they use on game shows to get rid of a losing contestant. "They just announced that Mr. Maroni's father died two days ago, and Mr. Maroni is moving to Cincinnati to take care of his mother."

contestant

"WHAT?" The first day of school is bad enough without getting hit with a massive curveball while you're still at your locker.

"Want to know who we have instead?" Matt asks.

I can't even begin to guess who'll be the master of my universe this year.

"Ms. McCuddles."

It's not that I dislike Ms. McCoddle—she's nice, young, and has super-blond hair—but Matt and I had her way back in kindergarten, and even though we're totally grown up now, she still thinks of us as kids. It was fine when we were five and she told us to call her Ms. McCuddles and hugged us when we fell during recess, but now we're almost embarrassed when we see her in the hall.

I try to analyze our new situation. "Option one—Ms. McCoddle is easy on us since she's used to dealing with little kids, and we won't have to plug in our brains all year."

analyze

Matt offers a different opinion. "Option two—she tries to make up for being a kindergarten teacher by being super hard on us."

"The one year we're supposed to get a guy teacher—figures something would happen to mess it up."

Our worst fears are realized when Ms. McCoddle walks by. "Derek! Matt! Did you hear the good news?"

We look down at our sneakers and nod.

"I'm setting up the mats and juice boxes now. Want to help?"

Matt and I stare at her like she's just asked us to run over the principal with our skateboards.

Ms. McCoddle laughs so hard, she snorts. "I'm kidding! We're starting right in on the Civil War. Get ready for some fierce discussion."

fierce

We watch her walk down the hall with a feeling of dread.

"Option two is officially in effect," Matt says.

I barely hear him because I'm halfway down the hall, looking for the janitor, hoping he'll agree to knock me on the head with a mallet to put me out of my misery.

Woe Is Me

hover

Carly and Maria are climbing out of their skins with joy. They had Ms. McCoddle back in kindergarten too and now hover around her desk like seagulls down at the pier looking for leftover food to grab.

The decorations in Mr. Maroni's classroom only make me miss him more. Photos of astronauts, bridges, gorillas, and fighting soldiers remind me how Matt and I were foiled by the school gods who insist on our continued suffering. I try to comfort myself by sneaking a peek at the Calvin and Hobbes book hidden in my desk, but even my favorite fictional friends can't jolt me out of my sadness today.

fictional

Ms. McCoddle tells the class she's wanted to move up to our grade for several years and Mr. Maroni's leave of absence will give her a chance to fulfill her dreams. I have dreams too—but mine consist of staring out the window and thinking about escaping. When I look over at Matt, he seems to be doing the same thing.

absence

Ms. McCoddle spends the first half hour talking about how she'll run the class, then sends us to the media center to choose a book for our free-reading time. As I head out the door, she pulls me aside.

"Ms. Williams told me how you used to illustrate your vocabulary words—are you still doing that?"

I tell her that Ms. Williams, the reading specialist, and my mother both forced me into it, but now it's a habit I almost enjoy. When I show Ms. McCoddle some of the illustrations I did this week, she thankfully does not get all cuddly but just nods her approval.

approval

Joe, who has been torturing me since first grade, waits for me in the hall.

"Trying to get in good with the new teacher by showing her your stupid little stick figures?"

I want to tell Joe he might take

some diet tips from my stick figures, but I don't feel like getting
thrown into the school trophy
cabinet.

"Anime—now those are real
drawings." He shoves the book he's
just taken out of the library into my
face.

I realize I'm taking my life in my
hands by correcting Joe, but I feel I
have to. "Actually, anime is when the
drawing moves," I explain, "like a
cartoon or movie. You know, like
'animate.' It's called manga when
it's a book. You should ask Matt—
he's an expert."

manga

Joe looks like someone has just
dropped a baby grand piano on top
of his crew-cut head. He searches
his cobwebbed mind for words but
comes up short; if the guy hadn't

humiliating

been humiliating me for years, I'd almost feel bad for him.

"Since when did you get so smart?" Joe asks. "I liked you better when you were a moron."

I want to tell him that I'm *not* smart, that my grades are usually horrible, and every bit of homework is a struggle. But I'm too busy trying to digest the words *I liked you better when*....I thought Joe was my mortal enemy, and now he's telling me he's *liked* me all this time? What's the next surprise—one of the lunch ladies wants to meet me after school to climb trees?

Matt has checked out lots of manga books; when I look through the stack, I realize he's read all of them before. My mind implodes with the thought that someone would actually read a book from

implodes

school more than once. I shake my head in amazement and wander to the next aisle.

I know most kids enjoy browsing through books in the media center, but it's always been one of my least favorite parts of school. Other students might glance through these shelves and be thrilled by all the different stories and characters; for me the spines of the books just stare back like a line of gangsters with machine guns loaded with ammunition. *You think you can read us, tough guy? Go ahead and try— we'll crush you.*

ammunition

As I scan the books to find one with the shortest chapters and least number of pages, Carly appears beside me and points to the book in my hand.

"Don't get that one," she says.

inspects

"The story's really slow, and the main character's boring."

She inspects the row of books in front of us and pulls out a volume. "This one's really funny—it's about a boy and his best friend. You'll like it."

I shrug and tuck it under my arm. I want to thank Carly for her help, but Maria and Denise are flittering around us like fireflies, and I need to get away from all that girl energy.

It feels like it's almost noon, but when I look at the clock, it's only nine thirty. Schools are on totally different time zones from the rest of the world; it's amazing how clocks slow down when they're hanging on a classroom wall. I'll have to ask Ms. Decker why we never study interesting things like that in science class.

What Gets Me Through the Day

When the bell finally rings, the teachers don't let you run out the door; they make you walk calmly, the same way convicts are forced to march around a prison yard.

convicts

By the time I race up my driveway, Bodi's instinct tells him I'm on my way, so he's pacing by the door. Because he's older, I'm gentler than I was a few years ago when I used to dive-bomb him in the doorway. I

instinct

stick my face into his thick fur, hoping if I inhale enough dog smell, the stench of school will start to disappear. I can't do that for long, though, because Frank is jealous and starts jumping up and down in his cage.

I have a monkey!

Frank is the capuchin monkey my parents finally let us adopt a few months ago after they couldn't take me bugging them anymore. (For anyone who thinks hounding your parents for something day and night is a bad strategy, I'm here to tell you—it's tried and true and works 99 percent of the time.)

strategy

Now Mom has a permanent reason for nagging: She tells me ten times a day that Frank is not our "pet" and that we are his foster home until he's old enough to enter "monkey college," where he'll be trained as a companion for a disabled person.

I got the idea to adopt a monkey from my friend Michael, who's in a wheelchair and has a capuchin named Pedro who helps him with daily tasks like changing water bottles, picking up things from the floor, and putting in DVDs. Frank can't do any of that cool stuff yet, but I'm confident that one day he'll be as talented as Pedro.

Even though my mother doesn't want me to take Frank out of his cage when I'm home alone, I can't resist a monkey in a diaper who's bouncing up and down to greet me. I unlock his cage and hand him a treat from the bowl on the counter. Mom made me swear a thousand times

maintenance

applicant

that I'd help with Frank's daily maintenance, but I still don't bother to see if his diaper needs changing. I don't care what I promised, changing a monkey's diaper is definitely not on my to-do list—today or any other day. Luckily, the only smell is Frank's normal monkey aroma.

The monkey organization makes an applicant go through a lot of interviews, and Mom said if I *really* wanted to adopt a capuchin, I had to fill out the paperwork myself. The organization wanted to make sure people would be around during the day and were pleased that my mother's office is next door and that my father works from home. The fact that my mother is a veterinarian and has taken care of Pedro for years didn't hurt either.

Believe it or not, the main obstacle to adopting a monkey was ME—the person who wanted one most. The organization won't approve a foster family if the family has children under ten because monkeys are as much work as little kids and they don't want the foster parents to be overwhelmed.

I kept telling the woman I was twelve, which is TOTALLY different than ten, but she still needed to think about it. My mother used this as a perfect opportunity for a "teaching moment," reminding me how immature I can be half the time. I told her that if my math was correct—which is unusual—that meant I was mature the *other* half of the time, which was about all a mother could possibly hope for.

immature

relented

mammals

The woman finally relented and said we could be a foster family for Frank. One of the volunteers brought Frank to L.A. and helped him settle in with us. It's only been a month, but Frank already feels like part of the family.

Bodi, Frank, and I climb into the pit I made by shoving the couch, table, and armchair together, and I realize that daydreaming about this moment with my favorite mammals is pretty much the only reason I made it through school today.

Outside, Here I Come!

After hanging with the boys for a while, I put Frank back in his cage, give Bodi a slice of turkey from the fridge, and grab my skateboard. A few years ago, I would let Bodi run alongside me as I rode, but now I try to conserve his energy.

conserve

Matt meets me at the top of the street, and we ride to our new favorite place—UCLA.

academics

Sure, the University of California at Los Angeles sounds like a weird place for two kids our age to go after school, but Matt and I don't go for the academics. This summer, while waiting for my mother to drop off some reports to a colleague, I discovered the college campus happened to be the most amazing playground in the city. I thought college meant studying day and night, but there were students everywhere riding bikes, skateboarding, and jogging through the campus. Since UCLA is just a few blocks from our neighborhood, Matt and I spent a lot of the summer there working on our moves.

Today we go to the marble stumps that are part of an art installation and we jump from one to another without stopping. After that, we leap to the wall of the parking garage and creep along the bricks, holding on with our fingertips. Matt just got a new camera with built-in video, so he takes plenty of movies of me climbing. Then he shows me how to use it, and I record him too. A few students stop to watch us as they go to class, but most of the time they leave us alone.

nerdy

But the person watching us now is not a nerdy student; he's a campus security guard.

"You kids signed up for classes here?"

Based on his question, I expect to see a grin on his face, but when I jump down from the wall, he isn't smiling.

"What if you kids get hurt, then what? Are your parents here? Do

identification

you have any identification in case you fall and need to be rushed to the hospital?"

Does this guy really believe Matt and I plan that far ahead? Hel-lo! Just as we're about to leave, a guy sitting on a nearby wall comes over.

"Jerry, these boys aren't going to fall—they have better balance than you do."

The man seems a little older than a college student and looks leaner and faster than athletes on TV.

gymnasium

"This campus is not a personal gymnasium—especially if people don't even go to school here." The guard looks over to Matt and me, but this time his expression doesn't seem so angry.

"Come on, Jerry, give the kids a break."

"Ahhh, I've got more important things to do anyway." When the guard leaves a few minutes later, he isn't angry at all.

I hold out my hand to the guy who saved our butts. He shakes it and introduces himself as Tony Marshall.

"You seem too old to go to school here," Matt says.

"I don't. I come here to do parkour."

parkour

Matt and I look at each other, utterly confused.

Tony laughs. "You kids are doing it already and don't even know what it's called." He puts down his back-pack and in one leap jumps onto the side of the brick building behind us. He inches along the top by holding on to the thin strips of concrete.

Matt videotapes while I hold my breath. Tony jumps from the corner of the building to the post eight feet away. Instead of climbing down, he bounds from the post to the bench.

"Whoa!" Matt checks his camera to make sure the video came out.

I'm speechless. Why can't *this* guy be our teacher?

obstacle

When we run over to the bench, Tony doesn't even seem out of breath. "*That's* what parkour is— getting around an obstacle as efficiently as possible."

efficiently

"Who are you?" I ask. "Some kind of superhero?"

Tony laughs. "Better than that. I'm a stuntman."

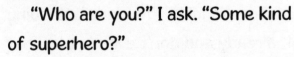

Real Life Gets in the Way of All My Fun

Mom and Dad listen to me talk about Tony all through dinner, but by the time eight o'clock rolls around, they've reached their limit.

Mom changes the subject by asking me how I like having Ms. McCoddle again. I tell her the universe just wants me to be miserable by giving me a recycled kindergarten teacher. She ignores me and

recycled

tells me she heard Mr. Maroni is doing well in Cincinnati. Dad grabs the new media center book from the counter and hands it to me.

"I've been looking everywhere for this," I lie. "Where'd you find it?"

"Propping up the crooked table leg in the den."

"I wonder how it got there?"

Mom takes Frank out of the cage; I pet him, then pet Bodi too. It might seem crazy, but I never want Bodi to get jealous now that we have another animal in the house.

"Speaking of reading, how about if we start the year off on the right foot and hire a tutor?" Mom suggests. "That way all of us can have stress-free homework time."

"Relaxing homework? What's next—happy funerals?"

"Derek!" Mom snaps.

It's just a joke, but after I say it, I realize other kids might actually *have* stress-free homework. I picture kids like Carly listening to Mozart with scented candles while they complete their assignments every night. Am I the only kid in class who crumples papers, bangs his head on the table, and gets sent to his room all because of a few crummy essay questions?

scented

My mother takes Frank next door to her office to change his diaper while my father looks over my math problems and nods his approval. Since it's still the beginning of the school year, the homework is easy. As much as having a homework tutor sounds like admitting defeat— *Yes, I need someone to stand over*

assignments

me like a two-year-old; yes, I need help staying focused; yes, I can go to the bathroom by myself—I wonder if it's something I should consider. Judging by the books Matt's brother Jamie had in our grade, the work will be getting harder by the day.

"Maybe Tony can be my tutor," I say. "He can help me to perfect my jumps."

"Not exactly what I was thinking, but nice try," Dad says.

"If I can't take stunt lessons, I guess I'll do the next best thing." I tuck the library book underneath the cushions of the couch and curl up with Bodi to watch an action movie on TV.

All I Want to Do

I don't know about Matt, but the next day at school I barely listen to Ms. McCoddle. While she's talking about the assassination of Abraham Lincoln, I imagine myself inching up the balcony of Ford's Theatre, grabbing hold of the velvet curtain, and swinging smack into John Wilkes Booth, knocking the derringer out of his hand before he shoots the

assassination

recommended

president. Who says a stuntman can't change the course of history?

"How do you like that book I recommended?" Carly asks me at my locker. "Does it have enough action for you?"

I tell her that not only haven't I read it yet, but I'm not even sure where it is. Her expression says she can't even *imagine* losing something as precious and magical as a book.

She tells me about the solar system project she's doing in Ms. Decker's class, but all I can think about is trying to jump from the wall to the bench at UCLA.

"I posted that video of Tony on YouTube." Matt throws his book into his locker. "He's my new hero."

When Carly asks who Tony is, Matt goes into a lively reenactment of yesterday afternoon. I notice he's

reenactment

written the word PARKOUR in large letters on his notebook.

Matt and I race to the door when the bell rings. Ms. McCoddle tries to get us to slow down, but we have more important things on our minds.

We spend the next several hours at UCLA climbing up walls and crawling along stairs like cheetahs. We both look around for Tony but don't see him anywhere.

I find a set of stairs and realize it might be possible to walk along the handrails instead of on the steps themselves. I plot the moves in my mind before jumping on the bottom rail to begin.

"Dude," Matt says. "It's a cement sandwich if you fall."

"I don't intend to." For some reason I've never been so sure of anything in my life. I walk all the way up

pivot

apprehensive

impress

five levels without looking down. When I get to the top, I pivot and walk back the other way. Matt videotapes the whole thing and is impressed when I land in front of him moments later.

"That was amazing!" he says.

"Come on, you try it."

Matt puts his camera down and follows me to the staircase, but I can tell he's apprehensive. I go first and take my time, offering encouragement along the way. He completes the first level but then jumps back down to solid ground. I make the decision to keep going on my own. When I get to the bottom, I hear the sound of slow applause, one person clapping. It's not Matt who's impressed this time; it's Tony.

"You planned your moves, then

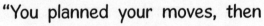

executed them to perfection," Tony says. "Just like the pros."

This is the first time in my entire life I'm getting credit for preparation, and I wish Matt had recorded Tony's praise so I could play it back for my parents over and over again.

preparation

Tony hands me his card. "Why don't you have your mom and dad give me a call?"

"So you can tell them what a good thinker and planner I am?"

He laughs. "No, so I can ask their permission to use you in a new movie I'm working on."

permission

Matt lowers his camera. "We've been extras in movies before," he says. "Derek and I were in crowd scenes on the boardwalk two different times."

"Being an extra is fun, but it's a

coordinator

petrified

lot of standing around." Tony bends down and looks me in the eyes. "But I'm the stunt coordinator for a movie shooting now with an actor your age and size who's petrified to do a similar move on film. I'm talking about you coming on set and doing something even easier than you did today."

Matt's eyes pop out of his head like a cartoon wolf when it sees a pretty girl.

"Do you mean..." I can't even finish my own sentence.

When Tony stands up, he looks like a sculpture of a lean muscle machine. "I'm talking about you, on camera, getting paid to do stunts."

I break the land speed record getting home.

Please, Please, Please!

Because my dad is a storyboard artist, I've been on movie sets plenty of
times. And if you live in Los Angeles,
you're used to films being shot around
the city on a regular basis. But being
able to jump and skateboard and
climb on camera takes my interest in
movies to a whole new level.

I shove another forkful of meat-
loaf into my mouth, then realize I

should use my best manners if I want my parents' okay. I even wait until I finish chewing before speaking again. "Maybe they'll light my clothes on fire and let me run through the middle of the promenade," I say.

My mother closes her eyes, which means she's trying to calm herself down before she answers. "When I spoke to Tony, he said he's only interested in you doing what you were doing on campus—climbing walls, skateboarding down the rail, that kind of thing. Minimal stuntwork."

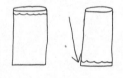

minimal

"Things some big-shot kid actor is too afraid to do," I say.

My father is still processing the fire remark. "You are *not* jumping off a bridge, lighting yourself on fire, or any other cockamamie idea.

cockamamie

Got that? These people are professionals. If you want to do this, you have to be one too."

I nod as if being mature is what I dream about at night.

"Tony gave me several references," Mom says. "The people who've worked with him give him high marks. And they'd only need you on set for a few days."

I drop my fork onto my plate, and the noise gives Bodi a start. "A few days? I thought I'd miss a month or two of school!"

My father laughs. "You'll probably have a day to rehearse and a few days to shoot. And the law requires a parent or guardian on set and three hours a day of schoolwork."

Figures that my parents could turn something as amazing as being a junior stuntman into a sad excuse for homework.

"What else?" I ask. "Tests, boring assemblies, and bad cafeteria food?"

"Tony's sending over the script for Dad and me to read before we decide. It's the story of a kid whose neighbors are aliens. One of your scenes takes place on a soundstage in Culver City made up to look like the neighborhood on Halloween. The other is on a set made to look like a junkyard."

Now this is more like it! Aliens, junkyards, and stunts? I shove the tutor and three hours a day of mandatory homework into a tiny corner of my brain and concentrate on how great this is going to be.

Just as I'm about to taste victory, my father wipes his mouth with his

mandatory

napkin and pushes his plate away. "If Mom and I agree to this, you know we're going to need something from you in return."

I'm afraid to ask.

commitment

"We're going to need a commitment on your reading. A promise to read and work on your vocabulary every single day."

As he talks, I try to remember if he and I have ever had a conversation that didn't include some kind of pep talk about reading. But this time is different. If they give their permission, I'll even promise to grow up and become a librarian—*that's* how much I want to be in this movie.

Weirdness with Matt

rumor

The rumor that a famous stuntman asked me to be in his new movie flies through the school. I'm the one who started the rumor, of course, but still it's nice to have some attention that isn't focused on my low grades.

Carly and I talk for a minute after art class while Maria and Denise giggle behind us—it's kind of lame but also kind of cool. When I see Matt stick his finger in his mouth to fake-vomit, I leave Carly and run down the hall to catch up to him.

"Your parents haven't even said yes yet," Matt says. "Are you sure you want to tell the whole school?"

"They're going to say yes," I answer. "They're just going to make me work for it."

"Tony was at UCLA other times too," Matt says. "He came over once, but I left before he could talk to me."

I'm not sure what Matt is trying to say. "Do you mean he wanted to hire you instead of me?"

Matt shrugs. "Why not? We both do the same routines."

I stop short in the hall and remind Matt that I had just walked up five levels of stairs on the handrails when Tony approached me.

Matt leans in close. "Are you calling me a chicken?"

"Why are you acting like this?" I ask. "Stop being such a jerk." Out of the corner of my eye, I see Carly watching us and am embarrassed to be seen in an almost fight with my suddenly aggressive best friend.

aggressive

"*You're* the jerk," Matt says. "Your scene will probably be cut from the movie anyway."

I'm stuck watching Matt's back as he hurries toward his locker.

"Deep down, I'm sure he's happy for you," Carly says. "He probably just wants to be in the movie too."

"How would you know?" I head in the opposite direction, leaving Carly in the middle of the hall alone.

It's almost like this meteor of negative energy crashed into the hall and ricocheted from Matt to me and then to Carly. But when I turn back to apologize, Carly's already gone.

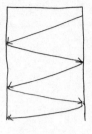

ricocheted

My Parents Lower the Boom

"Okay," Mom says. "Here's the deal."

I brace myself for what's coming.

"When you wanted to adopt Frank, that was the only thing in the world you cared about," Dad says.

"Homework, chores—nothing else mattered but getting that monkey," Mom adds.

The sinking feeling in my stomach tells me where this conversation is going.

"You agreed to take on some added responsibility, but once Frank arrived, you ignored all your promises." Dad's expression looks more serious than the bust of a president at city hall.

Mom leans back in her kitchen chair. "This pattern of desperately wanting things, then disregarding your end of the bargain is a bad habit that has to stop."

My parents have obviously forgotten what it's like to be a kid with no money, no car, and no power. Of course we say anything to get what we want—what else are we supposed to do? I feel bad they're out of touch with the way things work, so I continue to listen politely.

"The good news," Dad says, "is that we read the script and think the movie is fun and appropriate for

appropriate

45 ★

kids your age." He pulls the screen-play out of his bag. "Do you want to read it? Check out the story before you sign on?"

Great, more assigned reading. I tell Dad I'll definitely read it before we start shooting. Definitely maybe, that is.

"Also, we talked to Tony, and the three stunts he wants you to do are things you do all the time anyway. He reviewed them with us thoroughly, and Mom and I agree they seem safe," Dad adds.

"Does that mean yes?" All I want is for them to agree so this conversation can end.

"Your mom and I will have to sign lots of permission forms and releases if you do this," Dad says. "So we want you to sign something too."

My mother takes a sheet of paper from the folder on the counter. It's neatly typed and has a place for a signature at the bottom.

signature

"Is this a contract?" I ask.

"That's exactly what it is," she answers. "And it has three sections."

I bang my head against the kitchen table until my father makes me stop.

Mom continues. "I, Derek Fallon, agree to the following. One: I will change Frank's diaper once a day."

She looks up to gauge my reaction. All I can think about is *How badly do I want to be in this movie? Is it worth handling monkey poop?* After a few minutes of contemplation, I decide it is.

contemplation

"Okay," I agree. "What's next?"

"Not so fast," Dad says. "You

had agreed to help out with Frank before. This time, you're signing a contract. I suggest you read the fine print."

It seems like there's no way of getting out of this. I scan the paragraph entitled "Section One."

"This is outrageous!" I yell. "If I don't change Frank, you take away my skateboard? What if I forget?"

"Hopefully, signing your life away will help you remember." Mom moves down to the next section. "Two: I will read one book a month for fun."

"How can it possibly be fun if you're forcing me to do it?" I suddenly realize my parents' bodies have been taken over by aliens from another galaxy. If I don't escape soon, they will suck out my brains through my nostrils while I sleep. I make a beeline for the door.

galaxy

"You don't *have* to sign the con-tract," the dad alien says. "They'll just get some other kid to do the stunts."

I wonder how long before these aliens decide to conquer the rest of the planet and will finally leave me alone. "What's the third section?"

conquer

The mom life-form finally smiles. "Section three states that you agree to have a fabulous time on the movie."

This is obviously an intergalactic trick to try and get me to surrender, so I read the rest of the contract very carefully. Sure enough, the last section tells me to have fun shoot-ing the movie.

"Think you can manage Frank and some reading?" Dad says. "I don't think your mother and I are asking too much."

identical

Mom holds out the pen, and eventually I take it. I sign my name at the bottom of the form. Then Mom makes me sign an identical one so I have my own copy.

She hands it to me and shakes my hand like she's closing a business deal. "Congratulations, Derek. I'll call Tony tomorrow and tell him you can start rehearsals."

Inside I'm jumping up and down with happiness, but that still doesn't keep me from turning on the hallway light before I go to bed—in case my parents really *have* been taken over by aliens.

My First Day on Set

I text Matt to tell him I won't be in school for the next two days and am surprised when he doesn't text me back. On another day, I might worry that he's still mad and things are getting strange between us, but this is not just any other day.

Since the movie studio insists a guardian accompany kids under eighteen, my dad volunteers. (Mom

declines

concentration

has three feline surgeries scheduled so she declines.)

On the drive to Culver City, Dad gives me lots of advice, most of which consists of telling me to FOCUS. People have been telling me to focus my entire life, but always on schoolwork; it's weird to get concentration advice about leaping and skateboarding.

Tony greets us at the security gate and shows Dad where to park. Dad doesn't bring a sketchpad with him the way he usually does, which means he plans on watching me every second. Tony introduces us to the director, a woman named Collette with wild brown hair over-flowing from under her L.A. Dodgers baseball cap. Turns out she worked with Dad on a thriller a few years ago, and she tells him she looks forward to working with me too.

"You and Tony take as much time as you need." She bends down and gives me a wink. "As long as you're ready by tomorrow—9 A.M."

She laughs, but something tells me she's probably not kidding. Lucky for me, my job is to jump and climb, not study or read. As Uncle Bob says, "piece of cake."

We walk to the set, and Tony bounces up and down like we're boxers stepping into a ring. "Let me give you some background," he says. "The main character of the film—a kid named Chris—just got back from a Halloween party and hears strange noises at the neighbor's house. Chris runs outside to check, the director yells 'cut,' then you get in place. When Collette yells 'action,' you run across the yard and climb up this." Tony turns the corner and points to the tallest wall I've ever seen.

"What do you think?" he asks.

I don't answer because I'm already halfway up the wall.

What's Not to Like?

Surprisingly, Dad keeps to himself on the set. He sees a few acquaintances from other jobs and doesn't seem overly focused on me, which is a relief.

acquaintances

Tony appears happy with my climbing and gives a thumbs-up to the director when she comes by. He then drops me off in the wardrobe department to get fitted for clothes—the same outfit the actor will be wearing in the scene.

The costume designer's name is Zoe. She asks me what size I usually wear, and I feel like a moron when I tell her I don't know because my mom still buys all my clothes. She smiles and tells me her son doesn't know what size he is either, which makes me feel a little better, but not much. She measures me, then goes through several racks of different clothes.

When she comes back, I can't stifle my surprise.

stifle

"You want me to wear pajamas?"

"The character Chris is getting ready for bed and goes next door to check out the neighbors, right? Seems to me that calls for pajamas."

The tops and bottoms are a thick

cotton flannel, bright red and with a design of dog bones and leashes. They seem comfortable, and the dog theme reminds me of Bodi.

After I try them on, Zoe makes me stand on a box in the middle of the trailer while she makes adjust- ments.

adjustments

"Today's just the rehearsal," I say. "I can't wait to meet the actors tomorrow."

She mumbles something as she hems my pants, and I realize her mouth is full of pins and she can't answer.

"Tanya Billings is in this movie. She's great," I say. Tanya Billings used to have a show on the Disney Channel until she made an action movie last year that was a huge box office success. Now the magazines in my mother's waiting room have photographs of her doing normal things like riding her bike and going shopping. In this movie, I'm not sure what part she plays, maybe the sister of my character, Chris.

Thinking of Tanya Billings makes me think of Matt; we watched Tanya's last movie together at least four times. My relationship with Matt is like the ones I have with Mom and Dad, or Bodi and Grandma—always there, without a lot of thought or effort. There's no way a little fight like the one we had the other day could affect our friendship. If I get to meet Tanya Billings tomorrow, maybe I'll ask her to sign an autograph for Matt. He'd like that.

Zoe tells me my pajamas will be

relationship

ready the next day. She talks to someone on her walkie-talkie, then escorts me to the hair and makeup trailer. She introduces me to a man named Bruno, who checks my skin.

"I don't have to wear makeup, do I?" Between the pajamas and makeup, I wonder what I've gotten myself into.

"We don't usually worry about makeup with the stunt team," Bruno says. "If you guys are doing your job right, no one should see your face."

Bruno takes me over to the hair department where there's a shelf lined with Styrofoam heads wearing various wigs. He removes a long, dark brown wig from the stand.

various

"Why do I have to wear a wig and a witch's hat?" I ask.

Bruno seems confused. "Didn't

you read the script? Your character just came home from a Halloween party."

"Oh, yeah. I forgot." I guess being in a movie isn't too different from real life; I spend half my time pretending I've read stuff I haven't.

Bruno makes me sit in a chair, then places the wig on my head. He brushes and styles it with care, as if it's real hair and I'm at the hairdresser's. When he's done, he talks on *his* walkie-talkie to Tony, who tells him he's waiting with my dad at craft services.

As I follow Bruno across the set, I have no idea I'm about to discover the hidden treasure of a movie set.

It's Almost as Good as Christmas

"You mean there's free food on movie sets? Why didn't you tell me this before?"

My father shakes his head. "I've been keeping you away for this exact reason."

I walk through the trailer and don't know where to begin. Cake, brownies, cookies, muffins, soda, potato chips, bagels, hot chocolate, candy bars, gum, and M&M's—and that's just the first shelf. It's like scoring the biggest Halloween jackpot without having to dress up or knock on doors.

I take a huge bite of my first candy bar. "You mean I could've been eating free candy all these years?"

reserved

"The food is reserved for the cast and crew," Dad answers. "Not for the son of a storyboard artist. It's a long day working on a movie— the crewmembers need to refuel."

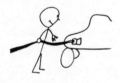

refuel

When I start to fill my pockets with licorice, Dad shoots me one of his looks.

"I'm refueling!"

Tony laughs and tells Dad it's fine. As if to join in the free food fest, Dad pours himself a cup of coffee.

I choose my next candy bar and

realize how much more bearable school would be with a craft services department. NOT the cafeteria ladies who stir big pots of brown stuff for lunch, but workers who lay out candy, cakes, and slices of pie in neat rows for kids to come by and take for free all day. In a perfect world, it would be located right next to our lockers so Matt and I could sneak in a quick snack between every class. Compared to this movie set, school now seems like the most horrible punishment on the planet, worse than being stuck on a chain gang with girls who won't stop talking.

If I were the type of kid who signed petitions and started a committee, this is TOTALLY the kind of project I'd put my time and effort behind.

committee

A Strange Silence

Four candy bars, two muffins, and three hot chocolates later, I almost need to be carried to the car.

"You think you overdid it, champ?" Tony asks.

I tell him I'm fine, but all I want to do is curl up on my bed with Bodi and sleep.

"You did a great job with the climb and the jump," he says. "But tomorrow's the real deal—will you be ready?"

"I've been ready my whole life," I say. "See you at 8 A.M. sharp."

I'm eternally grateful that my father doesn't spend the ride home yelling at me for indulging in too much sugar. Even though we take surface roads, the streets are clogged with traffic. Dad doesn't complain, and I begin to wonder if the aliens have returned to take over his brain again.

indulging

When my cell rings, I hope it's Matt so I can tell him about the free food and the stunts, but it's my mother asking if I had a fun day. I leave out the part about eating too many snacks and tell her I did.

"Well, that means you fulfilled clause number three in your

contract," she says. "That just leaves numbers one and two."

The thought of changing monkey poop when I get home makes me rush for the button to lower the window. The cool air feels good as I stick my head out of the car.

"Derek? Are you still there?"

I tell Mom I'm fine and we'll be home as soon as we can. I text Matt again but get no response.

"I bet Matt wishes he could be there tomorrow. He must be pretty proud of you," Dad says.

Since we're in rush-hour traffic that's not rushing, I decide to kill some time and confide in my father.

confide

"I thought Matt would've been happy too," I say, "but he's been kind of weird since this whole thing happened."

"Really? Why didn't you tell me about it before?"

"I'm telling you now." Yet again, the downside of being an only child: living under the parental microscope.

"I'm sure Matt could've done those stunts too," Dad says. "I'd say you're both about the same skill level, wouldn't you?"

"Well, yeah, but I'm definitely the one to try new things first. The day Tony saw me, I walked up five flights of stairs just using the rails."

gridlocked

"WHAT?" If we hadn't been in gridlocked traffic, I bet Dad would've pulled over the car.

"It was no big deal," I lie. "I do it all the time."

Dad calms down a bit. "I'm sure there were several reasons

Tony chose you. There's size to consider—Matt's about fifteen pounds heavier than you. The stunt coordinator needs to match the stuntman to the actor in terms of height, weight, and coloring. You could've gotten the job for those reasons too."

I stick my head back out the window. I liked it better when I thought I got the job because I was braver and faster, not because I was the right size.

When we finally get home, my mother hands me the phone. "Someone wants to hear all about your first day on the set."

I grab the phone and start to tell Matt about the wall and the free food. Except it isn't Matt who I'm talking to; it's Carly. I continue telling her about my day but it's with less enthusiasm than when I thought Matt was on the line. As we talk, I check my cell to see if there are any texts from Matt. There aren't.

Mom watches me lift Frank out of his cage and take him into the living room. She tells me I can hang out with Frank while she finishes cooking dinner. I take out my shoe box of miniature knights.

"Come on, Frank. Help me line them up on the table."

"It's not our job to train him," Dad says. "We're just helping him get used to living with humans."

They've told me this numerous times, but that doesn't stop me from wanting to teach Frank a few simple tricks. I mean, Pedro fills

numerous

Michael's water bottle; it seems only fair that I should get Frank to hand me a crummy old action figure.

irritation

When Mom calls us for dinner, I head for the kitchen.

"Derek!" Mom says with irritation. "Where's Frank?"

"He's okay. I'll get him." I go back, get Frank, and put him in his cage. It's not like we live in the rain forest—how much trouble can a monkey get into watching TV?

When I see the platter of broccoli and fish, I tell Mom I'm still full from eating on the set. She says okay and tells me to rest up for my big day tomorrow. Because my stomach hurt earlier, she gives me a one-time pass to get out of changing Frank's diaper and sends me upstairs with my library book.

Instead, I settle onto my bed with Calvin and Hobbes, my sketchbook, and my favorite markers. But even Calvin and Hobbes can't make me feel better tonight—I'm too busy checking my cell every few minutes. I realize I'm being ridiculous. Matt is my best friend. If I want to tell him about my day, I can just call him. Again.

"I had a great time on the set," I say to his voicemail. "You would've loved it. Call me."

I spend the rest of the night pretending to read and waiting for Matt's call.

Choke

This time Dad brings work to the set. I'm not sure if it's because he's on deadline or because he wants to pretend he's busy so he won't make me nervous. Either way, I block him out and focus on Tony.

"Scene 22—your scene—is first up today, which means you won't have to spend a lot of time hanging around waiting. Let's get you to wardrobe so you can put those pajamas on."

"Is Tanya Billings here today?"

"Dude, right now you need to concentrate on climbing that wall in as few takes as possible, okay?"

I suddenly realize that any mistake on my part could hold up this whole production. I look around the set at more than a hundred crewmembers—electricians, sound guys, cameramen, assistants, makeup artists, producers, people from the studio, the director—and grasp the reality of the situation. I'm a kid who slips up a lot; there's always some teacher or neighbor or parent who wishes I'd done things differently. I imagine a crewmember with one of those chalk clapperboards announcing every take. "Scene 22, take 1."

production

intensifies

scenario

"Scene 22, take 2." As I follow Tony across the set, the image intensifies: "Scene 22, take 87 ... take 135." Suppose I screw up and the director screams at me in front of everyone? Suppose they have to close down the movie and everyone loses their jobs? Before long, I am a few breaths away from a full-blown panic attack.

"Derek, are you okay?" Tony asks.

I tell him about the scenario I've just created in my mind.

"With that imagination, you should be writing screenplays instead of doing stunts! What are you worried about? No one's asking you to perform brain surgery. You're climbing a wall, you're running an obstacle course—stuff you do every day. All the director wants is for you to be you. You can't mess that up, right?"

My father magically appears next to us. It's as if his parent antennae alerted him that something was wrong from the other side of the set.

"You all right?" he asks.

"He's just got a case of the jitters," Tony says. "He'll be fine."

jitters

My father pretty much ignores Tony and looks me straight in the eyes. "You don't have to do this if you don't want to," he says. "They'll move on to another scene and find a new stuntboy. Happens all the time."

I can tell by the look on Tony's face that this is not the pep talk he was hoping for.

"On the other hand," Dad says,

"if you want to use your natural instincts and show these people what a twelve-year-old boy is capable of, I suggest you go on out there and kick some butt." He gives me a wink and holds open the door to the wardrobe trailer.

expectantly

When Tony looks at me expectantly, I realize the only person who would really get yelled at if I screw up is Tony. He took a chance on hiring me, and I'm not going to let him down.

"Give me a minute to get changed," I say. "I've got a wall to climb."

Star Power

The crew still isn't finished lighting the fake neighbors' house, so Tony and I go over to craft services.

He doesn't have to tell me to avoid temptation; I already plan on filling my pockets AFTER my stunts.

temptation

"Hey, you want to meet Tanya Billings? She's right over there." Tony points to a pretty girl in front of the muffins. I recognize her right away and hope he doesn't introduce us

bewildered

because I already know I'll say some-thing stupid.

But it's not seeing a big movie star that has me bewildered; it's what she's wearing.

Dogbone pajamas.

"Why is she wearing the same pajamas as me?" I whisper to Tony.

He seems as confused as I do. "Because she's in your scene. She's playing Chris."

"Chris is a GIRL?" I shout.

"I thought you said you read the script. Of course Chris is a girl."

This is what happens when you assume that if something is impor-tant enough, somebody will end up telling you about it. I can't blame anyone but myself.

My mind races through a million thoughts. What will my friends say when they find out I'm pretending to be a girl? Do I have any friends left? Why hasn't Matt called me back? Am I going to have to do any girl stuff? Does this mean I'm now a stuntgirl?

Then the news hits me: Tanya Billings is the biggest teen star in the world, and I'm doing the stunts she's too afraid to do! Girl stunts or not, it's still amazing.

When Tony brings me over to meet Tanya, I'm feeling pretty good about myself—until I have to open my mouth.

"I'm Tanya. You must be my stuntman," she says. "Or stuntboy. Whatever the word is."

stammer

I stammer what's supposed to be an introduction, but all that emerges is a series of grunts.

"I didn't get that," Tanya says. "What's your name again?"

What comes out next is the closest thing to *Derek* I can muster.

"Doc? That's a cute nickname. Nice to meet you, Doc." When she shakes my hand, her skin is soft and warm and feels like the bread my mom bakes when it comes out of the oven.

One of the production assistants leads Tanya to the set to get ready for her scene.

"That went well," Tony says.

"Really? You think so?"

"I'm goofing on you," he answers. "You were a mess! She's a twelve-year-old kid too—you don't have to be so nervous around her."

I tell Tony I won't be such a loser next time.

"Dude, there won't be a next time. She's the talent, you're the stuntboy. When they're filming your stunt, she's gone for the day or shooting somewhere else. I've worked on tons of movies. Sometimes I barely meet the actor I'm jumping off buildings for."

Tanya walks across the lot with an entourage of assistants and makeup people. She looks over her shoulder and gives me a wave. "Good luck on your jump, Doc!"

entourage

Like a knucklehead, I walk into a post as I wave good-bye.

The Jump

fiasco

"They're ready for you," Tony says. "All set?"

The fiasco with Tanya got me off track, but the cup of hot chocolate and raisin bagel with cream cheese helps get me back on course. The director comes over and puts her arm around me.

"If Tony says you're the boy for the job, then you're the boy for the job." She pats me on the head, which sends the hair and makeup people running over to spruce me up. I haven't been this fussed over since I was little and my mother used to try to beat down my cowlicks on school picture day.

cowlicks

The director shows me marks on the ground that she wants me to hit before I make it to the wall. "This way you'll be in frame—from the back of course." Tony and I run through the stunt one more time for the director to see. I start at the front steps of the house, jump over the wagon in the fake yard, vault over the table, and climb up and over the wall. After I'm done, I walk back around to the director.

"That was perfect," she says with a smile. "Do it just like that, and we'll get it in one take."

This is probably the only time in

monumental

horrified

my life I've ever done anything right the first time. When I look over at Dad, he's beaming. I'm glad he saw this "perfection" too so I'll have a witness to such a monumental event.

As I smile back at him, I realize the person he's standing there talking to is Tanya Billings.

When she sees me looking, she waves. "Go, Doc! Go, Doc! Go, Doc!"

I am horrified and run back to take my mark.

"Would you stop trying to impress her?" Tony laughs. "She was having a farting contest with the actor who plays her father yesterday. She's just a kid like you."

The thought of Tanya Billings of television and movie fame having a farting contest makes me laugh out loud, and when the director shouts "action!" I run through all the obstacles in the backyard and scramble up the wall as if aliens really *are* chasing me. I'm on the other side of the wall when the director yells "cut!"

The next thing I hear causes me to break into a giant grin—the crew is applauding.

"Great job, Derek." Collette turns to the assistant director. "I think that's a keeper."

The assistant director calls over to the camera assistant to "check the gate." I know from being on sets with my father that the cameraman or -woman needs to look into the camera to make sure no hairs or dust ruined the shot before the crew goes on to the next scene. All the crewmembers stand quietly and wait for the camera assistant.

"All set," she says.

"We're moving on, people," the assistant director says to the crew.

"The junkyard scene is in a few days," the director says. As she walks with me, three other people follow her, waiting to ask her a million questions. It's kind of like the director is the teacher and everybody else on set is a student. "Tony will give you a call to let you know when."

And before I get a chance to thank her for letting me be a part of her movie, she's whisked away by one of her assistants.

whisked

"You were amazing," Dad says. "One-Take Fallon. You want to go to craft services to celebrate?"

I try to catch a glimpse of Tanya Billings, but everyone has moved to another part of the soundstage to get ready for the next shot. My father guesses who I'm looking for.

"She was calling you Doc." Dad laughs. "I told her your name was Derek."

"You and Tanya Billings were having a discussion about me?" I'd sink into the ground with embarrassment if I weren't too busy trying to decide which candy bar to eat first.

"She had to prepare for the next scene, so she couldn't stay," Dad says, "but she asked what day you were coming back."

"She did?" Even shelves full of candy bars are not as important as this extraordinary news.

extraordinary

"She did." Dad's grin is so wide, I can see the silver fillings on his back teeth. "I think she likes you."

I can't decide if I'm horrified or thrilled to be having this conversation with my dad. On the drive home, I make him repeat his conversation with Tanya Billings fifty times.

Back to Reality

When I get home, school is still in session, so I go to Mom's office to tell her about my stunt. I wait until she finishes examining the dachshund with the bladder infection, then tell her how I met Tanya Billings and how I needed only one take.

dachshund

"I found something I'm good at," I say. "Something I can do without support and reminders every five minutes."

reminders

antiseptic

My mother washes her hands with the antiseptic soap as she talks. "Please don't tell me you're thinking about this as a career! Stuntmen have shoot-outs and drive cars a hundred miles an hour. You're not going to grow up and do that for a living, are you?"

How did the conversation go from "I'm so proud of you" to "you can't do that!" in less than five seconds?

"I just wanted to tell you about my day. Sheesh."

"Well, it sounds wonderful. And I'm glad you're back early because one of the tutor candidates is coming at four. You can let me know what you think."

The artificial world of the movie suddenly seems like the best possible

candidates

place to live. No homework, no tutors, no worried parents—just free food, stunts, and pretty movie stars with soft hands.

"Can you see if Frank needs to be changed?" she asks. "He seemed a little sluggish this morning. I want to make sure he's okay."

sluggish

Mom stands by the door with her file folder and calls the next patient. A woman in the waiting room grabs two cat crates from the floor and hurries into the examination room; she looks like she's rushing to catch a plane with armloads of luggage.

Before she follows the woman into the room, Mom turns to me. "See you in a few hours, Doc."

It's one of those parent comments that's funny and not funny at the same time.

communicating

I head into the house to check on Frank, hoping I'll have some time to myself before school lets out and the tutor arrives. I check my cell to see if Matt texted me. He didn't. It's probably the longest we've gone without communicating unless one of us was on vacation.

I decide to take things into my own hands and wait for him at his house after school.

Can Someone Tell Me
What's Going On?

I see Matt walking down the street before he sees me. When he does, I'm relieved to see him smile.

"How'd it go?" he asks.

"I had a blast. I left you texts and a voicemail—did you get them?"

relieved

He nods. "Yesterday was nuts. You know the parking garage at UCLA? I tried climbing up the side and fell. That guard was furious. My leg is bruised, but nothing broke."

"You've never even done the bottom row of that garage—I can't believe you tried to go all the way up. Were you by yourself?"

He nods again.

"We said we wouldn't do parkour without someone else there. You could've gotten hurt. Why are you acting like such a daredevil?"

daredevil

"What—I'm the scaredy-cat, and you're the big, bad stuntman? You think you're the only one who can climb twenty-foot walls?"

"No, of course not. You just need to be careful."

"Are you giving advice now?"

I'm wondering if the aliens who abducted my parents have now replaced my best friend with an envious android. I try to steer the subject back on track by telling

android

Matt about Tanya Billings. I even tell him Tanya asked my dad when I'd be back on set.

"She did not!" Matt jumps off the stairs and throws his backpack into the air. "Can I meet her too?"

I tell Matt that I asked Tony the same question, but he said no visitors on set. Matt sits back down.

"Who does she play in the movie, your character's sister?"

"Uhm, actually, she *is* the main character. She plays Chris."

Matt seems confused. "You're doing stunts for Tanya Billings?"

"Sure am." And pretty proud of it too.

"You're doing stunts for a GIRL?" Matt collapses onto the ground with laughter. "Why didn't you tell me you were playing a girl? That's hilarious!"

"I'm not *playing* anything," I say. "I'm not an actor. I do her stunts."

"Yes, but when you climb over that twenty-foot wall, you're doing it as a girl, right? That's beautiful." He pulls out his cell and starts texting.

"Who are you texting? No one cares!"

"Joe and Swifty will love this," Matt answers.

"I miss two days of school, and you start hanging out with those knuckleheads?"

transferred

We've known Joe since first grade; Swifty is a kid who transferred to our school last year and lives next door to Carly. He's got a sick sense of humor and walks so slowly, Matt and I nicknamed him Swifty his first week here.

"Why on earth would you do

stuff with them?" I ask. "They don't even skateboard." As soon as I say it, I realize how stupid it sounds: Matt and I have been friends since way before we started skateboarding. He's always meant more to me than someone to ride with.

"Swifty's dad manages a storage facility down by the highway. You should've seen us running through this huge warehouse of crates. I even sat in a forklift. It was *real*, a hundred times better than a movie set."

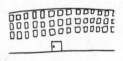

facility

Matt picks up his phone on the first ring. "I'm with the stuntboy," Matt says. "He's doing stunts for a GIRL."

"Not just a *girl*," I grumble. "Tanya Billings."

"I guess they needed someone

petite

physics

petite," Matt continues. "Someone Tanya Billings's size."

"Why are you doing this?" I ask. "You're wrecking everything!" I jump on my board and head down Matt's driveway.

"See you tomorrow," Matt calls. "Stuntgirl!"

If I ever make it through middle school and end up taking high school physics, I hope the teacher explains the universal principle of how a day can go from being the best you've ever had to the absolute, total worst.

You Thought That Was Bad . . .

By the time I get home, I'm still stunned. When Matt won the mountain bike at the church raffle last year, I was happy for him. When his father's friend invited Matt to a Lakers playoff game, I thought that was great too. Why can't he be glad when something good happens to me?

Nothing exhausts me more

stunned

pondering

than pondering these kinds of questions, so I walk in the door and collapse on the couch. All I want to do is rub Bodi's belly. But a twenty-something-year-old guy with black nerdy glasses is sitting at the table drinking iced tea with Mom. I figure he's one of her vet interns until I realize she's using her mom voice and not her doctor voice. Which means he's here for the tutoring job.

"Derek," Mom says, "meet Ronnie. Ronnie, Derek."

He gets up to shake my hand and knocks over his iced tea. As my mother scurries for a towel, Ronnie blushes and gives a little shrug. I didn't think it was possible to cause more spills than I do; maybe this guy is okay.

Mom asks me to show Ronnie

scurries

the sketchbook with my vocabulary drawings. He laughs when he sees them and shows me his own notebook with lots of lightning bolts and wizards in the margins. I'm not sure if Mom's impressed, but any guy who draws instead of paying attention in class is all right with me.

As Ronnie discusses what days he's available, I lift up the piece of fabric covering Frank's cage. He's been very quiet since I got home, and now he's just lying there. I ask Mom if he's okay.

available

"I usually won't take him out of the cage when there's a stranger here—monkeys really prefer to be with people they know—but he does seem sick." Mom cradles Frank in her arms like a baby.

"You have a monkey?" Ronnie asks. "That's so cool!"

"You can't hold him," I say, "but you can pet him if you want."

Ronnie reaches over to pet Frank just as Frank leans his head back and hurls. Not just a little dribble— big, projectile stuff that lands all over Ronnie and everything on the kitchen table.

projectile

"Derek, get a towel from the bathroom! Ronnie, I am so sorry!" Mom quickly puts Frank back in the cage to clean up Ronnie and the kitchen.

Frank is moaning, Mom is apologizing, Ronnie is wiping off vomit from his shirt, and all I'm thinking is, For once, this has nothing to do with me.

"Well, I guess this is the last place

you want to work now," Mom tells Ronnie. "I can't say I blame you."

"Are you kidding?" Ronnie asks. "I just got puked on by a monkey— I guarantee things can't get any worse."

guarantee

"Uhm . . . I wouldn't hold my breath," I say.

Mom shoots me a giant piece of MomMad and turns to Ronnie. "You mean you're still interested in the job?"

"Sure." He turns to me. "If Derek approves, of course."

As much as I don't want to spend a few hours a week with some stranger standing over me while I read, Ronnie seems pretty cool, and I say yes. He washes his hands and face before he leaves, then says he'll see me on Thursday.

After he's gone, Mom opens Frank's cage. "I'm going to give him a quick exam. There's definitely something going on."

I hold open the door for Mom and hope everything's okay with my monkey.

Oops . . .

When my mother comes back in the house with Frank forty-five minutes later, she's not happy. She places him gently in his cage, then motions for me to follow her to the office. Her silence makes me think something's wrong, so I take a mental scan of all the things I've done since I've been home and, thankfully, come up empty.

Most of the time, Mom's veterinary office is jammed with people and their pets, so I like it when it's after hours and everything is quiet. She leads me into the first examination room, turns on the light panel mounted to the wall, and puts up an X-ray.

"Are those Frank's insides?" I ask.

"Yes." She points to a spot that's almost the size of a quarter. "What do you think that is?"

radiologist

I stare at the circle as if I am now a radiologist. "A tumor? Does Frank have cancer?"

"It's inside his stomach, but I don't think it's a tumor." She looks at me with her Most Serious Face. "Did you let Frank play with anything he wasn't supposed to?"

"No! You told me never to give him things he could swallow. He's *my* monkey too—I don't want him to get sick."

"Fair enough. Did you ever leave him alone with any of your toys?"

"No—I already told you." I've barely finished the sentence when I remember lining up my knights on the living room table the other night before dinner. "I left the room for only a second! He couldn't have."

I run back inside the house and take down my box of small action figures from the shelf. The blue knight, the red knight, the green knight with the mace . . . I dump the box onto the floor to make sure the whole set is there. I realize with a sinking feeling that the horse with the red banner is not with the others.

"Are you missing any?" Mom's

voice is so calm, it scares me more than if she were yelling.

I check under the living room couch and table but don't find it. "The horse is gone. Do you think Frank swallowed it?"

"We'll find out soon enough. I just paged Melanie to come assist me. Whatever's in Frank's digestive system is too big to pass. I'm going to have to go in and get it."

I close my eyes and lean against the wall. This morning I was on a movie set doing stunts, talking to a movie star. By the end of the day, my best friend's making fun of me, I have a homework tutor, and my mother's going to cut open my adopted monkey to retrieve my horse. How do these things happen? I put all these questions on hold to

retrieve

deal with my mother's wrath. Except she isn't furious; she just seems sad.

wrath

"When I tell you something like 'keep the toys away from Frank,' I don't say it to ruin your fun. I say it to keep Frank safe."

"Is he going to die?" Out of all the questions in my mind, it's the only one I care about right now.

"Hopefully not, but he's in distress. He hasn't eaten in several hours, so operating now is the smartest thing."

distress

"Are you mad?"

She shakes her head sadly. "I'm not mad. I just wonder when some of your listening and paying attention skills will kick in."

I don't admit it's something I wonder about too.

"Can I be with Frank while you operate?"

"That's not appropriate, but you can help me prep him."

I've lived with a vet long enough to know what that means.

abdomen

"Come on," she says. "I'll let you shave his abdomen."

Under normal circumstances, I'd ask if I could give him a mohawk or do his back in stripes, but I'm grateful she's not furious, so I don't say a thing.

Even when you include shaving a monkey, this still might be the worst afternoon of my life.

A Horse of a Different Color

Before Frank's operation, I ask Mom if I can take the day off from school tomorrow to take care of him. She tells me I already missed two days this week for filming and insists I go. She's been incredibly supportive about the fact that I almost killed our monkey; Dad, on the other hand, is using all the discipline he has not to explode like an angry volcano.

supportive

blockage

He places the horse Mom took out of Frank in the middle of the table. "Do you see why we asked you to keep your toys away from Frank? Do you see how something like this could cause a blockage in his digestive system?"

I nod yes, but most of my energy is focused on my toy horse. Frank's stomach acids must've tried to break down the plastic because the horse looks a bit worn. I want to pick it up and examine it but realize this would push Dad past his breaking point.

"We're going to have to tell the people at the monkey placement organization about this. They might decide we're not a good foster family and ask us to return Frank."

Dad didn't need to tell me this.

Losing Frank is all I've thought about since this happened.

He rushes to the side door to let Mom in. She's carrying Frank, who's bandaged and still groggy.

groggy

I ask Mom if I can hold him. My expression must look pretty sad because she says yes.

I sit on the couch and she lays Frank in my lap like a newborn baby. I want to hold him close to me but know he needs to be treated with care.

"I'm sorry," I whisper into his ear. "I'm really, really sorry."

It's probably just my imagination, but it seems that when Frank looks at me, he smiles. Of course, it might just be the drugs from the operation. I hold him for a long while until Mom takes him to the kitchen to give him water with an eyedropper. The horse with the red banner still stands in the center of the table as if he's guarding a fort for one of my knights. I throw him into the trash can and bury him under the coffee grounds and orange peels.

My Own Kind of Stardom

I ask Mom another fifty times if I can stay home to watch Frank, but she drives me to school anyway.

"You haven't been in class for two days," she says. "You must be excited to see Matt."

For some reason, almost losing Frank yesterday makes me spill my guts to Mom about what's going on with my best friend. I tell her Matt hasn't been himself since I got hired for the movie.

"I only have two more stunts to do, and part of me wants to just get it over with so things can return to normal. But another part of me is furious with him for not acknowledging that I've just done something cool."

acknowledging

"Matt's been under a lot of pressure," Mom says. "Jamie hasn't worked in months and just hangs around the house sleeping. His mom is really worried, so I'm sure that's affecting Matt too."

Jamie is Matt's older brother who's had lots of jobs since he graduated: he's been a clerk at the DVD store in the mall, a waiter at the coffee shop in Westwood Village, a dishwasher at the vegetarian restaurant on Wilshire, and even mowed lawns

vegetarian

for Carly's mom at her landscaping company. Last time I saw him, it looked like he hadn't showered in a week. When I said something to Matt, he told me he didn't want to talk about it.

"Still, Jamie having problems is no reason for Matt to make fun of me," I say.

"I agree. But people don't always do things that make sense, do they?"

I know she's right, but some of the sadness and anger from yesterday's encounter still remains.

encounter

"Remember when you were mad at Matt a few years ago because he planned his birthday party at the bowling alley on a day you couldn't go? You two worked through that, didn't you?"

If I'd known the ride to school

psychiatrist

torturous

was going to turn into a therapy session, I would've stretched out on the backseat and pretended it was a psychiatrist's couch. Besides, I don't see how reliving a torturous event back in fourth grade will help Matt and me get back to normal—which is all I really care about. I tell Mom I'll be back right after school and race to my locker before the bell.

Carly, Maria, and Denise are waiting for me.

"Did you meet Tanya Billings?" Carly asks. "She's in the movie, right?"

"I love her," Denise says.

"Her movies are *amazing*," Maria adds.

I open my locker and throw in my gear as if it's another normal day. "Yeah, I met her. We hung out for a while—she's really nice."

Maria and Denise actually start

jumping up and down like they're on pogo sticks. Thankfully, Carly calms them down.

excruciating

They make me tell them about Tanya in excruciating detail, and as I do, three girls turn into five, then eight, then twelve right before my eyes.

"Okay, what's going on out here?" Ms. McCoddle asks. "Everybody into the classroom."

Carly tells Ms. McCoddle what we've been talking about.

"Maybe Derek can write a report about his day on a movie set and present it to the class," suggests Ms. McCoddle.

I panic at the realization that two days off from school could lead to extra work. "I'd love to, but I already told everybody everything. There's nothing left to write about."

"Did you tell them you're doing stunts for a girl?" The smirk on Joe's face makes me want to hide inside my locker.

Carly stops snapping her gum. "You're Tanya Billings's stuntperson?"

Before I can answer, Swifty interrupts. "Must be nice skateboarding with a wig on."

I don't think I've ever had a conversation with Swifty—so why is he suddenly acting like an expert on me?

"Is that true?" Carly asks. "Did you have to wear a wig to pretend you were Tanya?"

I look around and notice Matt. He's got a huge grin, the same one I've seen on his face a hundred times, usually when he's anticipating one of us making an awesome jump.

But right now I don't feel like he's waiting for me to land on my feet; this time, he wants me to fall.

I don't intend to.

"Tanya is *great*," I say with bravado. "But she's too afraid to do the obstacle course and climb over the wall, so that's where I come in."

bravado

I turn to Carly. "You should've seen us on the set yesterday—both wearing matching pajamas with these dogs all over them—hanging out at craft services—that's what they call the trailer with all the free food. She was really supportive. When I was doing my stunt, she was standing with my dad, cheering me on from the sidelines. She already gave me a nickname—she calls me Doc. She asked my dad what day I was coming back so she could be there."

lasso

Carly, Maria, and Denise go crazy, and I manage to lasso Joe and Swifty too. Joe asks me all kinds of questions about the free food, and Swifty wants to hear more about Tanya Billings. If Matt had some jealous plan to embarrass me for filling in for a girl, it didn't work. For the rest of the day, everyone asks me about being on the set.

At the end of school, I want to talk to Matt about something normal like Frank swallowing my horse to see if that will make us friends again. But Matt's running down the hall and out the door—with Swifty and Joe by his side.

Reading Circle

I thought for sure Mom would cancel my tutoring session with Ronnie so I could take care of Frank, but when I get home, Ronnie's in the kitchen skimming through my library book.

"Boys, animals, skateboards—this looks good."

Maybe if I ignore Ronnie and the book, they'll both go away. I go to the cage to check on Frank, but it's empty.

"Your mom said to tell you Frank is with her in the office today."

I head to the door to go see him, but Ronnie shakes his head. "You know what I like to do?"

"Get puked on by monkeys?" I ask. I know I'm being rude, but the last thing I feel like doing after working hard in school all day is doing more work with a tutor.

Ronnie doesn't seem offended in the least. "No, I'd rather try and choke them with my toys."

boomerang

Whoa! Ronnie's insults come back to me like an evil boomerang. "It was an accident," I say. "You weren't even here."

"No, I was home preparing for today's session." He pats the seat of the chair next to him. "We're going to start with my favorite activity—reading out loud."

"I haven't done that since third grade."

"The reason you don't do it isn't because it's babyish—it's because you're embarrassed to read in front of your classmates."

I suddenly hate Ronnie and wish Frank weren't recuperating so he could throw up on him again.

recuperating

"That's why I'm here," Ronnie continues, "to get you to be a better reader so you *can* read out loud in class. Come on, we'll take turns."

He opens the book and starts reading the first paragraph. I don't interrupt him, hoping he'll keep going and finish the entire chapter. To my surprise, he does.

Afterward, he hands the book to me. "Your turn."

I do what I always do—look ahead to see how many pages are in the chapter.

Ronnie stops me. "It doesn't matter if there are three pages or thirty. Just read."

What kind of planet is Ronnie on? Of course there's a difference between three pages and thirty! Twenty-seven, to be exact.

After a few moments, I look up to see if Ronnie is bored or frustrated with my reading, but my slow pace doesn't seem to bother him. He motions for me to continue, but I'm distracted by someone running up the driveway. To my surprise, Matt bursts into the kitchen with his videocamera.

"My mom just told me about

distracted

Frank swallowing the red stallion. Is he okay?"

I tell him Frank is all right but my favorite horse action figure didn't survive the operation. I introduce him to Ronnie, then ask if we can cut our session short so I can hang out with Matt. I don't tell him my best friend and I have been having a difficult time lately, but I'm hoping Ronnie will take pity on me anyway.

He doesn't.

"We still have another half hour to go," Ronnie says. "Why doesn't Matt do his homework while we finish?"

Matt and I both laugh, knowing there's no way he brought over his homework. It's the first normal friend moment we've had since the day Tony hired me.

"I'll go over and film Frank," Matt

hiccup

says. "Then maybe we can ride down to the village."

It feels like a huge weight's been lifted off my shoulders. I guess Mom was right; our fight was just a weird hiccup that all relationships have once in a while. I pick up the book and start reading, hoping the rest of our tutoring session goes by quickly.

When I stumble on several words, Ronnie makes me slow down even more. To my ears, I sound like a second-grader, but he encourages me to go on.

After each scene, Ronnie asks me questions about the characters and the story. I visualize the story in my mind like a movie, the way Margot—a camp counselor I once had—taught me to do.

"Very good work," he finally says. "I'll see you next Tuesday, okay?"

Before Ronnie's even packed his bag, I'm out the door looking for Matt. I ask Mom's receptionist if she's seen him, but she says he left. I check on Frank, who's sleeping, then run out to the street to see if Matt's on his board. When I don't see him, I send him a text.

Matt texts back with:

ddn't wnt 2 interrupt. mom called 4 dinner.

I answer back that it's no problem and I'll see him at school tomorrow. I'm a little disappointed we didn't get a chance to hang out, but I'm happy that things are okay. And when Tony calls to tell me they're filming my stunt next Thursday, the world finally seems a little less worrisome.

worrisome

The Fame Game

slalom

At school the next day, I'm surprised when Principal Demetri asks me to come to his office. I figure this might have something to do with someone—I'm not saying who—setting up a slalom course behind the school with the orange traffic cones from the parking lot. But the principal wants something else.

Mr. Demetri introduces me to the two people in his office. The woman wears jeans and carries a notebook.

"This is Mary Souza from the paper. She wants to do a story about your junior stuntman work."

"I write about movies," Mary explains. "I thought this might be a good local-interest story." She points to the man beside her. "This is Bill Hernandez. Do you mind if he takes some photos?"

I want to suggest that Bill take some pictures of the slalom obstacle course, but I don't have my board with me today. But Bill says he wants photos of me doing normal things like being at my locker or eat- ing in the cafeteria. I'm flabber- gasted when Mr. Demetri writes me a hall pass and tells me to give Mary all the information she needs.

flabbergasted

As Bill takes a photo of me getting

camouflage

books out of my locker, I can see everyone in the classroom straining to look through the window next to Ms. McCoddle's door. Carly waves and smiles, but I'm more focused on Matt. He's sitting behind her and can't camouflage his disgust. *This wasn't my idea,* I want to say. *Mr. Demetri asked me to do it.*

While Bill runs out to his car, Mary and I sit on the chairs outside the media center to talk. She asks how I got involved in the film, what I liked best about being on set, and if I met Tanya Billings. She ignores the many calls coming into her cell and takes notes as we talk. As much as I'm happy for the attention, I'm a little embarrassed when our class goes down to the art room and everyone stares. Matt's in the back of the line, making faces with Swifty and Joe.

When Mr. Demetri asked me to do this, I felt special and important. Now, I just feel uncomfortable and wish the interview was over.

"One last question," Mary says. "If you had to do it again, would you?"

"It's been the best experience of my life," I lie. "I've never had so much fun."

Hurray for Hollywood

sentry

Bodi seems to know that Frank's been through some trauma because since the operation he hasn't left Frank's side. He sits next to Frank's cage like a sentry and doesn't realize the only person Frank needs protecting from is me.

My mother checks the paper each morning, and when it comes on Sunday, she's the first one to spot the article in the local section.

"This is wonderful." She leans against the kitchen counter and drinks coffee as she reads. "You sound so grown up." She spreads the paper out on the table so Dad and I can read it too.

I break my own rule about reading on the weekends and check out the article—photos and captions first.

"Really nice quote from Tony," my father adds. "He says you were professional and prepared."

I ask my parents if we can scan that sentence in the printer and enlarge it a hundred times so I can hang it in the kitchen to point to every time they think I'm messing up.

enlarge

"You should be very proud." It's not really an answer to my question, but Mom seems happy enough that I can probably talk her into anything.

As I put my dishes in the sink, I'm shocked by what I see on the windowsill. It's the toy horse that almost killed Frank.

"What's this doing here? I threw him away!"

"I pulled him out of the trash," Mom explains. "I thought he might serve as a reminder."

"Of how Frank almost died?"

She shakes her head. "No. That actions have consequences."

Even on a day with a glowing newspaper article about Yours Truly, my mother can't resist another teaching moment.

She rinses out her coffee cup and tells me it's no big deal and that the horse looks good next to her

consequences

collection of tiny cacti. I decide to take her at her word and drop the subject.

cacti

After breakfast, we go to the Hollywood Hills, where we take Bodi off the leash and let him trot alongside us as we hike. I walk ahead of my parents to my favorite part of the canyon, the caves. Sometimes there are tourists taking pictures because this was one of the locations used in the old *Batman* TV show. I imagine a crew here many years ago filming the Dynamic Duo in their Batmobile zooming out of this cave to fight crime. The actors probably weren't even here. I bet they saved the hard stuff for their stuntmen.

We avoid the puddles, and when we come out of the cave, we look

exhilarating

back in the other direction. The letters of the HOLLYWOOD sign stand guard over the canyon like giant white soldiers. I've lived here my whole life, but it's still exhilarating to see such a famous landmark up close.

My mother bends down to give Bodi some water. "Does the sign seem like it applies to you a bit more since you've been in a movie?"

I make a face like that's the stupidest thing I've ever heard, but in reality I was thinking the same thing. To celebrate the newspaper article, we stop at House of Pies, and I order a slice of chocolate cream. My parents split a piece of custard pie and let me choose which songs to listen to on the drive home.

When we get back, I sit on the

couch with Frank and Bodi and watch one of the action movies Tony sent over to show my parents his work. In one scene, he jumps off a bridge and lands in a tugboat full of garbage bags.

"Don't get any ideas," Mom says.

"Don't get anything *close* to an idea," Dad adds.

It's kind of a perfect day, one of the best I've had since summer—until I realize tomorrow is Monday and the school week's about to start all over again.

You Did What??

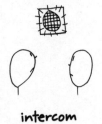

intercom

The next day, Mr. Demetri congratulates me on the article. I do appreciate his support, but I wish he had told me in the hall instead of on the intercom during morning announcements.

Ms. McCoddle applauds when he's done, and the class joins in—even Matt, which makes me happy.

On our way to the cafeteria later,

Joe walks alongside me with a book. He reads the words with painstaking slowness. Because I want to have teeth left to eat my lunch, I don't comment on his reading skills, which appear to be worse than mine.

painstaking

Swifty joins us and starts reading over Joe's shoulder, stumbling over every word.

"What's going on?" I ask.

They both laugh and head to the lunch line.

I grab Matt. "What's wrong with Swifty and Joe? They're acting like idiots."

"Like idiots—exactly." He gives me a friendly punch in the arm and walks away.

I must look pretty confused because Carly comes over and asks if I'm okay. I tell her I have no idea what Swifty and Joe are doing, but whatever it is, it's not funny.

"Matt too," Carly says. "Don't let *him* off the hook."

"What are you talking about?"

"What are *you* talking about?" She pauses. "You mean you haven't seen it?"

"Seen what?" I try to imagine the worst: that Swifty and Joe have taken yesterday's newspaper article, drawn a mustache on my photograph, and hung it outside the classroom.

"Come on."

I follow Carly to the media center, where she asks Ms. Myers if she can undo the Internet block for a few minutes. (This is what life is like when you're a girl who reads books in her spare time—teachers will do the impossible for you.) Ms. Myers tells her she'll give us five minutes.

Carly goes to YouTube and types in "IDIOT READER." I lean toward the monitor and am shocked by the video that starts to play.

deliberately

It's me reading out loud, slowly and deliberately. The video was shot from our porch and shows Ronnie and me sitting at the kitchen table. Watching the video is one of the most humiliating moments of my life.

"I *do* sound like an idiot," I say.

"Lots of people have a hard time reading, not just you. Who do you think posted this?"

It's a question I don't have to ask because I already know the answer: my best friend with the video-camera.

It's Over

I race to the cafeteria and scan the room for Matt. "How could you do that to me?" I ask.

"Hey, you're the one trying to be a big shot, with your movie and your newspaper article. I was just trying to help you out." Matt takes a giant swig from his carton of milk.

"By calling me an idiot?"

"That video's already gotten more

than five thousand hits—stop com-
plaining. I'm helping you in your quest
to get famous."

quest

"I don't want to be famous."

"You could've fooled me."

I have a sudden desire to pick up
his bowl of disgusting beef stew
and throw it at him.

"It's probably not five thousand
different people," Swifty adds. "I'm
sure some people watched it over
and over again."

I ignore him and return to Matt.
"If you were going to upload a video
of me onto YouTube, why didn't
you use the one where I'm walking up five flights of stairs on the
handrail—something *you* were too
afraid to do?"

defensive

Swifty and Joe laugh and Matt
gets defensive. "I wasn't afraid. You

were just so busy showing off, there wasn't any time left."

Joe pretends to read from a book in his bag. "I ... can ... do ... lots ... of ... stunts," he taunts.

taunts

His impersonation of me isn't what hurts—it's how hard Matt is laughing at the joke.

impersonation

I turn to face my ex–best friend. "Maybe you could've done some stunts too—if you didn't have to race home to babysit your twenty-three-year-old brother." I normally would *never* use Jamie as a weapon against Matt, but with our friendship over, hitting below the belt almost seems fair. "Or was that the time he didn't come home for a week and your parents didn't know where he was?"

Swifty and Joe look at Matt to

see if these things about Jamie are true. Matt looks almost wounded by my comment, and for a second, I feel bad.

"*You're* the loser," he shouts, "not Jamie!" Matt dives across the table at me, and the two girls on the other end jump out of their seats.

"Whoa! Calm down!" Mr. Walsh, the gym teacher, grabs Matt. "Save your tackling for phys ed, unless you want to spend the rest of the afternoon in Mr. Demetri's office."

"He started it!" Matt points an accusing finger at me.

Swifty and Jo chime in. "It was Derek!"

"It was not!" I say.

"I don't care *who* started it. It's over." Mr. Walsh ushers Matt back to his seat and stands behind him for several moments. Matt, Swifty, Joe, and I keep quiet until he leaves.

Matt finishes his milk and squashes the carton. "You better get to the media center before class starts," he says. "Take out *Goodnight Moon* before someone else does."

When I storm out of the cafeteria, it feels as if the entire room is laughing behind my back. A few days ago, I was worried about people on the movie set making fun of me; I never once thought I'd be ridiculed in my own school. By my best friend!

ridiculed

I duck into the restroom next to the nurse's office and lock myself in a stall.

I can't remember the last time I cried, but I make up for it now.

An Unexpected Friend

I use the rest of the lunch period to wash my face and get it together. For a minute, I think about going home sick but don't want to give Matt, Swifty, and Joe the satisfaction. I keep my head down and race for the door when the bell rings.

I decide not to say anything to my parents; just thinking about the sad look on Mom's face if she watched the YouTube video is enough reason to keep quiet. I didn't get a chance to eat at school, so when I get home, I wolf down my sandwich, feeding the crusts to Bodi. Then I get Frank out of his cage and take him and Bodi up to my room.

As painful as it is, I use my father's laptop to watch the video again. It's not news that I've always had trouble reading, but now it feels like a real disability. The more I watch it, the more broken I feel. And when I think about losing my best friend on top of it, I want to hide underneath the comforter Grandma made and never come out.

I ignore the knocking on the back door, hoping whoever it is will go away. When the knocking continues,

disability

I scoop Frank up in my arms and go downstairs.

Carly stands outside on the step and points to the monkey in my arms. "This must be Frank! He's so cute!"

I roll my eyes and let her inside. "I know you want to hold him, but monkeys are strange with people they don't know. I don't want him to bite you."

"Yeah, I don't want him to bite me either." She moves her hand toward his head. "Can I pet him?"

I tell her she can if she moves slowly. She smiles when she touches Frank's fur. I tell her it's okay to pet Frank but she can't forget about Bodi. She gets down on the tile floor and places her face next to Bodi's as she rubs his belly. He looks so happy, it almost makes me glad Carly came over.

"I thought we could go to the video store in the Village and see if any good DVDs came out this week."

Carly and I have never done anything like this, which immediately makes me suspicious. "You don't have to hang out with me just because Matt and I aren't friends anymore."

suspicious

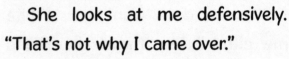

She looks at me defensively. "That's not why I came over."

"Yes it is."

defiant

She puts her hands on her hips, even more defiant. "I came over because I didn't want you sitting around thinking about that stupid video."

"That's kind of hard to do when eight thousand people have already seen it."

"It was only five thousand," Carly says.

"Well, now it's eight. Not to mention how many viewers wrote comments about what a moron I am."

Carly continues to pet Bodi's belly. "Is there any way we can take it down?"

I tell her we'd need Matt's password, which I don't have.

"Can you guess what it is?"

I run up and get Dad's laptop, and Carly and I attempt several different word and number combinations with no luck.

combinations

"This is all because of Swifty and Joe," Carly says. "They couldn't care less about Matt, but he's trying to impress them anyway."

I close the computer and ask Carly if we can talk about something else. I should've figured she'd want to talk about Tanya Billings—what she looks like up close, what she was wearing, neither of which I paid much attention to.

While Carly grills me, Tony calls to give me updates on the next day's schedule. Carly jumps up and down in the kitchen with fervor, pointing to herself. I shake my head no, but she doesn't stop.

fervor

"Would it be okay to bring a friend?" I ask Tony.

He pauses before he answers. "It's probably not appropriate because you'll be working. I hope she won't be too disappointed."

"I didn't say it was a girl."

Tony laughs. "But is it?"

Instead of answering, I tell Tony I'll see him tomorrow.

Carly is still jumping and pulling on the sleeve of my T-shirt. "Well? Well?"

"I wish I could, but I can't. Sorry."

We put Frank back in his cage and go outside to set up traffic cones in the backyard. We go into the garage and get the wheelbarrow, cooler, and stepladder too. We place them all around the yard in a tight course and spend the next hour running and jumping over the obstacles trying to beat each other's times. I had no idea Carly was so agile.

agile

My mom comes out after her last patient and brings us lemonade and mini cupcakes. I don't really think about the video or Matt the entire time Carly's here, and when she leaves, I really mean it when I tell her I had fun.

An Embarrassing Moment, Thankfully Not Mine

This time Mom accompanies me to the set. She insists we leave early so we won't be stuck in traffic. When she asks if things are better with Matt and me, I say yes, even though they're anything but.

She gives our names to the guard at the gate, who talks about the weather for a few minutes before letting us in. Tony finds my mother a chair, then asks me if I can do a few run-throughs before the director arrives. I tell him I can't wait.

I follow Tony's lead and take several moments to examine my surroundings. The soundstage has been transformed into a giant junkyard, complete with fake rust, dirt, and discarded appliances. Together Tony and I plan the best route around the obstacles.

discarded

"If I start at the bathtub, then go around the statue and over the dented motorcycle, I can land on the mini trampoline and leap over the picnic table before climbing the fence. What do you think?" I ask.

Tony smiles. "That's exactly how I'd do it too."

One of the production assistants tells Tony that the director is on her way, so Tony brings me to my mark, moves aside, and tells me to give it a go.

I take a running start to jump over the bathtub. Except I miss.

My mother gets up from her chair to see if I'm all right. I'm grateful she doesn't come running over like she used to when I was little.

misjudge

"Misjudge that jump?" Tony lends me his hand and pulls me out of the bathtub. "You okay?"

I tell him I'm fine and climb out. My mother moves her reading glasses up to the top of her head, which means she's now going to be watching me full-time. I head back to my mark and begin to run, but Tony stops me.

"Remember what we talked about the day I met you at UCLA?

Parkour is about making your way around obstacles. Whether it's a set of stairs or a problem at school, you need to plan the most efficient way around the hurdle." He pans the artificial junkyard with his hand. "Take a good look, then implement your plan."

implement

I try not to focus on the growing number of crewmembers watching us and concentrate instead on the best route to my goal. Tony reminds me to put safety before risk. This time when he tells me to go, I run, leap, and climb like it's the most natural thing in the world. When I'm done, he meets me at the fence and shakes my hand.

"Let's see if you're still One-Take Fallon today. But no pressure—take as many tries as you need," he says.

Tony introduces my mom to Collette, who is wearing red high-top sneakers, tights, and a hooded sweatshirt. Assistants hover around her with cell phones and coffee while she tells my mom how professional and smart I am. Mom nods politely, probably thinking about how I almost killed our monkey too.

When Collette yells "action!" I make the same mistake I made during rehearsal and land like a giant whale inside the tub. Tony and the director run over to see if I'm okay, but the only thing that hurts is my pride. I panic briefly when one of the assistants changes the chalk clapboard to SCENE 43, TAKE 2 but when it's time to go again, I sail through the junkyard heap like a pro.

The director shoots a few more

times from different angles, and I
nail it every time. She thanks me
profusely and tells the crew to set
up for the next scene.

profusely

"Who knew all that jumping off
the roof of the garage and swinging
on the zipline would prepare you for
your first job?" Mom pulls me in for
a hug, then thinks better of it when
she sees all the people around. She's
finally catching on that I'm too old
for that kind of affection.

Tony calls us over. "Tanya's shooting the next scene. You want to check
it out?"

I look at Mom, who says she's
happy to stay as long as I want. We
follow Tony across the set to the
fake backyard where Tanya sits
under a tree with the actress who's
playing her mother. The three of us

stand behind the director and out of Tanya's view.

"You ready?" Collette asks Tanya.

She nods and then Collette yells, "Action!"

"Chris," the actress mom says, "you have to stop talking about aliens. You're starting to worry me."

"I'm telling you," Tanya says, "they've moved indoors."

Collette yells, "Cut!" and she approaches Tanya. From where we are, I can hear her directions.

"The next line is 'They've moved next door.' You want to go again?"

Tanya nods. When Collette goes back to her place, the actress gives Tanya a wink and a smile, but her brow is furrowed.

furrowed

The clapboard reads SCENE 31, TAKE 2. Tanya blows the line again. And again. And again.

Collette tells the crew to take a five-minute break and goes over to Tanya.

"What's going on?" Collette asks softly. "What do you need?"

My mother gives me a nudge that means it's time to go but I am riveted to my spot.

riveted

"It's hard to memorize so many lines," Tanya says. "I've read the script a million times, but I just can't remember all the words."

The director holds out her hand and lifts Tanya to her feet. Then the actress playing the mother gets up too. "Let's all go to your trailer and read the scene together," Collette suggests.

Tanya nods and they walk over to the trailer on the edge of the set.

"See?" Mom whispers as we walk

to the car. "You're not the only one who has a hard time with words."

I don't need her to translate what this means. Tanya Billings, teen mega-star, has something in common with ME!

Awkward . . .

Ms. McCoddle obviously doesn't know that Matt and I are no longer friends because she tells us we're partners for the class history project. When she calls out our names, I expect Matt to sneer, but instead he just looks quiet and sad.

sneer

She passes out a timeline worksheet and tells us it's due by the end of class. I pretend to look for my pen to buy myself some time before I have to face Matt.

"I took the video off YouTube," he says. "You were right—it was mean."

I could just accept his apology, but I still feel pretty angry that he posted it at all. "What made you change your mind? Did Swifty and Joe get bored with you already?"

Matt shakes his head. "It's like making fun of somebody in a wheelchair trying to get down a curb or laughing at someone's misfortune. It's just not funny."

misfortune

"You thought it was funny the other day."

He traces the doodles on his desk while he talks. "I don't know.... With Tony picking you instead of me, I just felt left out. Then everyone in school had to make such a fuss."

He looks like he's going to cry, and I know how that feels. I want to do anything to have him be good old Matt again, so I tell him it's okay. His face lights up just as Ms. McCoddle approaches our desks to tell us to get to work.

"It wasn't just that you were making fun of me. You could get in a lot of trouble for posting videos without someone's permission."

"Believe me, I did. My dad was furious."

I don't say anything, but inside, I'm not unhappy Matt got yelled at.

As we collaborate on the work-sheet, I change the subject and tell Matt about Tanya Billings on the set yesterday. "It's not just me," I say. "Lots of kids have a hard time studying."

"No," he answers. "It's mostly you."

He shoots me a giant grin, and just like that, things are back to normal with my best friend.

An Idea

When I get home from school, I'm greeted by not only Bodi and Frank but my parents' copy of our contract, lying on the kitchen table.

My dad points to the contract and then points to Frank. After a moment, I realize what he wants.

"Frank's probably fine," I say. "Mom changed him this morning."

"His diaper's not fine," Dad says. "And I've been saving it for you."

heinous

As soon as I protest, Dad directs my attention again to the contract. I carry Frank to an empty examination room in Mom's office and begin the heinous task of changing my monkey's diaper. Just as I'm about to tell one of Mom's interns that I forgot how to do it and ask if she can help, Mom appears. Her right eyebrow is raised as she leans inside the door frame to ensure I finish the job.

"Very good." She hands me a plastic bag for the dirty diaper, which I can't get rid of fast enough.

"The woman from the capuchin organization called to check on Frank," Mom says.

"You didn't tell her about the horse, did you?"

"I had to. He's had major surgery.

She wasn't too happy and wants to reevaluate his placement with us."

"I don't want to give him up," I say. "What do we have to do to keep him?"

reevaluate

"You're going to call her," Mom answers. "And ask her that very question."

Out of all the teaching moments my parents throw at me, the worst is talking to grown-ups about my mistakes. Whether it's apologizing to Mr. Parker for using his faucet to fill up water balloons or telling Mrs. Donaldson that I didn't really mean to dig up part of her yard when I built my skateboard ramp, Mom's insistence on "personal responsibility" has never been anything but embarrassing. And now she wants me to call someone three thousand

insistence

miles away and beg her to let me keep my monkey?

Just when I think things can't get worse, I walk next door to find Ronnie waiting on our porch.

"Did you forget about our appointment?" he asks.

appointment

I hate that my house is no longer a safe place from schoolwork.

"Well, *I* didn't forget. Let's start by reading out loud where we left off last time."

"Oh, no!" If I tell him about the YouTube video, my parents will definitely find out, and now that things are okay with Matt, it hardly seems worth putting them through that.

"Okay, then, how about doing some of your drawings?" Ronnie says. "You can illustrate the story as we read."

I've been so busy with the movie these past few weeks that I almost forgot about my sketchbook. I get it from my room and flip through the pictures of my recent vocabulary words. Then I get an idea.

I tell Ronnie I'll be right back and find the movie script in my dad's office. I still haven't read it but scan through the ninety pages until I find scene 31. Sure enough, there are the words Tanya was trying to remember yesterday.

"You want to illustrate a screenplay?" Ronnie asks. "Shouldn't we be working on your book from school?"

I slowly read through the scene, then turn my sketchbook sideways. I draw several panels like a comic strip and follow that with figures acting out the story. Ronnie suggests a few ideas but mostly lets me be. When I'm done, I rummage through my pack to find the shooting schedule for the rest of the week, then illustrate those scenes too.

"You did good work today," Ronnie says.

sarcastic

I look up from my drawings to see if he's being sarcastic, but he appears to be serious. He says good-bye to Frank before he leaves and tells me he'll see me on Monday.

When Dad comes in to start dinner, I ask him if he'll do me a favor.

I hold up my drawings and the script. "Are you going to be near Culver City tomorrow? Can you drop these off at the set?"

My father puts down the eggplant and looks over my work. "Sure. I'm happy to."

I put the drawings in an envelope and address it to Tanya Billings. Then I add a note.

> Tanya,
>   Here are some drawings of your upcoming scenes. Maybe you can use them, maybe not.
>   Good luck!
>   Derek (a.k.a. Doc)

Then I put the envelope on the front seat of my father's car so he won't forget.

An Evil Plan

Matt meets me at my locker as if nothing bad ever happened between us. "What did the lady say about Frank?"

"She's in town for some big presentation, so she's coming over Friday night before she flies back to Boston. Mom told me we should have Frank's things ready in case the woman decides to take Frank back with her. I can't imagine never seeing him again."

Swifty and Joe wrestle their way down the corridor toward us. Matt and I exchange looks; neither of us wants any trouble.

One thing I know I won't be when I grow up is a psychiatrist because I can never figure out what makes people tick. For some reason, Swifty has the crazy idea that I stole Matt away from him, so he spent this week trying to slam my locker door on my hand or swipe my skateboard as I pack my bag with books. I got my board back, but all the drama just seemed like a giant waste of time.

drama

"How are you ladies doing today?" Swifty asks.

Joe tries to shake his bangs off

his forehead, but he's so sweaty, they don't budge.

When Matt and I don't answer, Swifty hits Joe on the arm and they head down the hall.

"They scare me sometimes. I don't know how you ever hung out with them."

Neanderthal

"If you pretend you're a Neanderthal, they're kind of fun." Matt leans against his locker. "Which brings us to the subject of your particular primate. How about if Frank isn't there when the woman comes to your house? Then she *couldn't* take him."

"Where else would he be? My mom's office is right next door— she'd definitely find him."

"Maybe he's not at your mom's office. Maybe he's somewhere else." Matt shoots me his most evil grin.

"What if you leave the back door open tomorrow and I sneak in and take him? In his cage, I mean. To keep him safe."

"Are you kidding? My mom would flip. *Frank* would flip."

"You said the woman has to catch a plane, right? All we have to do is hide him until she has to leave for the airport. She's not going to miss her flight back home. Then you call her the next day and say you and Frank were visiting Pedro and you're sorry you missed her."

Listening to Matt's plan, I realize how much better life is when he's on my side. As I close my locker, I discover Swifty and Joe lurking around the corner.

lurking

"Are you guys spying on us?" I ask. "Get a life."

Joe makes a move toward me, but Matt tells him to get lost.

"I think you should really consider Operation Hide Frank," Matt continues after they leave. "I'll take good care of him, I swear."

I don't have to think about it twice. "There's no way I'm putting Frank through that kind of trauma. Even if it means losing him."

Matt stops walking and looks me in the eye. "Is it because you don't trust me and think I'll take him for real?"

"No! It's not that...." I try to finish the rest of the sentence but can't. After a moment, I try again. "You really hurt my feelings before, but that's not why. I just want to do the right thing for Frank."

Matt smiles as he heads into

class. "We'll figure out another way. You're not going to lose that monkey."

And because Matt's my best friend, I believe him.

Back on Set

I've been hanging around craft services trying to run into Tanya Billings, but two doughnuts, three sodas, and two candy bars later, I still haven't seen her. I wonder what she thought of my drawings and if they helped her learn her lines. The nice woman who's been feeding me snacks all morning says she isn't sure if Tanya's shooting today. I adjust my wig, which is pinned into place. I still can't get used to being in drag to do my stunts.

Because Dad thinks I haven't been holding up my end of the bargain in the reading department, he asked Ronnie to tutor me today while I wait for my scene. Ronnie's never been on a movie set, so he walks around in disbelief at all the activity.

disbelief

"There are hundreds of people working on this movie. It's like a city." Ronnie nearly collapses when a green alien lurches toward us.

"I've been sitting in the makeup trailer for five hours," Tony says. "What do you think?" He twirls around like a Martian model.

"Cool!" When I touch his slimy scales, my hand recoils. "That's disgusting!"

recoils

"It should be," Tony says. "The guy doing makeup on this film is the best in the business."

I introduce Tony to Ronnie, who looks afraid to shake Tony's hand. I ask Tony what stunt he's doing this morning.

"I chase Tanya through the house," he says. "Then tomorrow, she lights me on fire."

Tony gives me the details of the alien's fate, but all I'm thinking about is that Tanya must be on set today. As if my imagination conjures her up, she appears beside me.

"I thought you were done," Tanya says.

I tell her today is my last day. Then I introduce her to Ronnie, who starts frantically combing his hair with his fingers. He finally gets hold of himself and gushes hello.

frantically

Tanya pulls me aside. "I liked your illustrations. They actually helped me to remember my lines."

"That's how I learn my vocabulary words." I open my pack and take out my sketchbook. Ronnie comes over all smiles as if he did the drawings and invented reading too. I shoot him a look that says *leave us alone* so he walks away and consoles himself with a candy bar.

consoles

Tanya flips through my book. "These are great." She takes out a script from her own pack. "It was such a good idea that I decided to do my own drawings."

I look through her copy of the script, and my heart sinks. Her illustrations are ten times better than mine—no, a hundred times better. They're funny and sophisticated and perfectly drawn. I was going to ask

sophisticated

her if she wanted help illustrating her next scenes but realize the last thing she needs is assistance from my little stick figures. I tell her the drawings are amazing.

"Your idea—I just copied it." She reaches for my hand and gives it a squeeze before heading back to her trailer. "I'll catch you later."

A dozen thoughts race through my head: Tanya Billings just held my hand! My illustrations helped her! Why does her hair smell like cinnamon? What does she mean she'll catch me later?—it's my last day on set. How does she plan on seeing me again?

I must look like I've been hit by a stun gun because Tony the Alien waves his hand in front of my face. "Earth to Derek! Earth to Derek!"

I shake myself out of my Tanya Billings trance.

trance

"The life of a stuntman," he says. "When the movie ends, so does your relationship with the actor you're doing stunts for."

I watch Tanya disappear into her trailer, hoping she'll turn around one more time to wave good-bye.

She doesn't.

A Different Kidnapper

I pick up my phone on the first ring.

"I went to your house to see Frank," Matt says.

"I told you monkey-napping was out of the question!"

"I wasn't going to take him, I swear," Matt says. "I wanted to check on him after the operation, but he was gone."

"Look in my mother's office. Maybe

she took him with her so he wouldn't be lonely."

Matt says he'll call me right back.

"You ready to hit the books again?" Ronnie asks. "You still have several hours until your scene."

To get out of reading, I ask Ronnie if we can watch Tony shoot his scene first.

obligation

"You've got an obligation to do your work," Tony says. "You signed a contract, remember?"

I answer my cell on the first ring. Anything to change the subject.

"Carly's here," Matt says.

This day is getting more confusing by the second. "What does Carly have to do with anything?" I ask.

"She saw Swifty at his house, and he had Frank! He and his cousin

imbecile

are taking him to where his dad works."

"What? Why?"

"Because he's an imbecile—how many more reasons do you need? I ran over to tell your mom, but she's not there. What should I do?"

"Monkeys can bite," I tell Matt. "Doesn't Swifty know that?"

"This is all my fault," Matt says. "If I hadn't hung out with Swifty and told him about your monkey, this never would've happened. He probably overheard us yesterday and let himself into your house."

"Never mind about that. We just need to get Frank back or the woman from Boston will take him for sure."

"Jamie's not doing anything," Matt suggests. "I'll see if he can drive me over."

I hear him talking to someone else in the background. "Carly's coming too," Matt finally says. "Can you meet us there?"

I don't want to blow my scene but tell Matt I'll find a way.

"How much time do I have before you need me?" I ask Tony.

He looks over at the clock in the next trailer. (I guess aliens don't wear watches.) "They're shooting your scene in three hours."

"I'll be back by then." I grab Ronnie and tell him that there's an emergency and I need a ride.

"Whoa, whoa!" Tony says. "You can't leave like that."

In all the confusion, I forgot I'm wearing the wig and girl sweats I'll need for my last scene.

"A friend's in real trouble," I tell Tony. "I'll be back soon, I swear."

Tony thinks about it a moment. "I'll call you to check in. Just make sure you don't leave me hanging!"

Just as I'm about to go, I notice Tanya's returned. "What are you doing now?" she asks. "I've got a few hours off. Want to watch a DVD in my trailer?"

convince

This is, by far, the best offer I've ever had in my life. For a second, I try to convince myself that Matt and Carly can get Frank back by themselves, that hanging out in Tanya's trailer is a choice any reasonable kid would make. But the thought passes quickly. Frank is my responsibility; it's up to me to get him back.

"I have to go," I tell Tanya. "Some jerk at school stole my monkey."

"If you don't want to watch a movie with me, just say so," she says. "You don't have to make up some ridiculous excuse."

"It's 100 percent true." I suddenly realize we're both wearing the same pink sweats, sneakers, and have long dark hair—like a freakish pair of twins. "You want to come?"

She calls over a guy who talks to the assistant director on the walkie-talkie. "As long as you're back by two," he warns.

Tanya and I drag Ronnie reluctantly to his car to be our chauffeur.

chauffeur

Just Like in the Movies

As we head toward the storage facility from different parts of town, Matt texts me directions. Even though we're in a hurry, Ronnie is very careful to stay under the speed limit. When we get near the warehouse, I text Matt for an update; he says they'll be there soon.

This is more action than Ronnie bargained for, and he seems relieved when I suggest he wait in the car.

I race into the giant warehouse. "Hello!" I yell. "Anybody home?"

Frank starts screeching when he hears my voice.

"Give me back my monkey. He's not a toy or a pet—he's an animal that can bite." The last sentence sounds like it came straight from my mom's mouth.

I spot Swifty just as he's about to open the door to Frank's cage. "Joe's coming soon. He's going to love this little guy."

"Don't do it," I yell.

"He likes me," Swifty says. "I can tell. Besides I wore a long-sleeve shirt to protect myself."

"Like a T-shirt is going to stop a monkey bite. What's wrong with you? What if he bites your face? You'd be disfigured for life!"

I look around the facility for

disfigured

Swifty's father, who can hopefully talk some sense into his son.

"Nobody's here to help you," Swifty says. "They're all at a meeting in the next lot."

Tanya's been standing behind me, but now she steps forward. "Is that Frank?"

Swifty performs a better double take than any professional actor could ever hope for. "Are you Tanya Billings?"

Tanya's probably been asked that question a thousand times, yet she smiles and nods as if it's the first. "Yes, I am. Nice to meet you."

As Swifty scrambles toward Tanya, he lets go of the cage door. Frank races out of the cage and past Swifty.

"Stop him," I yell. "He can't get loose!"

I race toward the cage, but Frank is already halfway across the giant warehouse.

"You idiot!" I tell Swifty. "We're never going to find him in here."

The last thing on Swifty's mind is locating Frank in this labyrinth. He's standing next to Tanya, swaying back and forth like a two-year-old. But I can't worry about saving Tanya from Swifty's stupid questions—I have to find my capuchin.

labyrinth

When I hear Matt's voice, I shout, "Over here! You have to help me."

Matt and Carly race toward me. Matt bursts out laughing when he sees my outfit, but he's even more shocked when he spots Tanya Billings. He skids to a halt with so much force, his sneakers leave rubber marks on the concrete floor.

Before Matt can fight with Swifty

about who gets Tanya's attention, Carly grabs him by the arm. "We're really big fans," she tells Tanya, "but right now we have to help Derek."

"That's why I came too," Tanya says.

Carly, Tanya, and Matt hurry to the middle of the warehouse, where I've finally located Frank. When Swifty joins us, I tell him to get lost.

"This is all your fault," I say. "You broke into my house."

"The kitchen window was open."

"You took Frank—who's not even mine, by the way. We're just a foster home." I try to get Frank's attention while I talk.

Swifty looks disappointed, as if the plan he'd worked so hard on is disintegrating before his eyes. I

disintegrating

wonder if he's acting sorry to impress Tanya, but it looks as if his remorse is genuine.

remorse

"I just wanted to feel included," Swifty says. "You and Matt are such good friends. I've never had a best friend like that—ever."

"And you thought kidnapping Derek's monkey, who, by the way, is being trained to help disabled people, is how to make friends?" Matt asks.

"There he is!" Carly points to Frank sitting on a giant crate at least thirty feet up on rows and rows of industrial shelving.

"Derek's right. This is my fault," Swifty confesses. "I'll get him."

"You'll scare him even more." I count the levels of shelves from Frank to the floor—five. Tony would be proud of how I map out my route before I begin to climb.

"Be careful!" Carly and Tanya say at the same time.

I move to the right and climb into the cab of the crane.

machinery

"If anything happens to the equipment," Swifty shouts, "my father will kill me!"

"You should be worried about Derek, not the machinery," Carly says.

misstep

I hop from the crane to the third shelf. I'm more than twenty feet off the floor; any misstep and I could get seriously hurt. But just like climbing the wall in the movie, I focus on where to put each foot next.

"Here I come, Frank. I'm taking you home." I pray that Frank isn't too frantic with all this activity and so many new people.

The last several feet are the scariest; I will myself not to look down. Finally, I'm close enough to get a good look at Frank. He seems terrified.

hoist

I hoist myself up until I'm sitting on the highest shelf. The ceiling is only about six feet away.

"Hey, buddy. You okay?" Frank must really be scared because even though I'm wearing a wig he scrambles up my arm and holds on to me for dear life.

I look down to gauge how far I climbed and am shocked when I see the others far below. I'm even more surprised to realize Matt is taping me.

"What are you doing?" I ask. "I'm wearing girl's clothes!"

"Dude, you were great! I had to tape it."

Carly, Matt, and Tanya are all smiles; Swifty just looks relieved.

I reach up and pet Frank. "You ready to head back down, buddy? Hold on tight."

I check out the route down and decide it's safer to inch my way across the top, then descend at the end of the row. I take my time— which is actually a new skill for me— and finally reach the ground several minutes later. Everyone wants to *oooh* and *ahhh* over Frank, but I hold him against me until he's safely back in his cage.

"This is more fun than making a movie," Tanya says. "You don't have to worry about messing up on camera."

"Unless your best friend's a cameraman."

Matt waves his camera in the air.

Carly runs to the restroom to fill the water bottle in Frank's cage, and I realize how helpful she's been through all this. She may have been the class Goody Two-shoes all these years, but lately she's turned into a reliable friend.

reliable

I answer my phone on the first ring.

"Where are you?" Tony says. "There's only one more scene before yours—get back here!"

I ask Matt if he and Carly can take Frank to my house. Luckily, Jamie's driving his parents' SUV, so there's plenty of room.

"Wake up!" I say to Ronnie, who's sound asleep in the front seat when we jump into the car. "We have to get going."

"Your parents are paying me overtime for this," Ronnie says. "Gas mileage too."

Tanya calls over to Matt and Carly. "Hey! Why don't you come with us to the set so you can watch Derek do his final stunt."

"Frank needs to get home," I say.

Jamie pipes in. "I'll take him back. Matt and Carly can go with you."

"Are you sure?" When I place Frank's cage in the back of the SUV, I feel bad for making fun of Jamie a few weeks ago. He's happy to see me and eager to help out with Frank. Even though he's going through a tough time, he's still the same old Jamie I've always liked. I thank him again for taking Frank home.

"Do you really think it's okay if they come to the set?" I ask Tanya. "Tony told me no visitors."

Tanya smiles. "I don't think anyone will give us a hard time."

Matt and Carly climb into the backseat of Ronnie's car, and I suddenly realize Swifty's standing in the parking lot alone. He's been the source of my suffering since school began, but I know what it's like to be left out, and even though he stole my monkey, I almost empathize with him now.

empathize

"You guys take off. I can't go anyway." Swifty shyly motions toward Tanya. "But it was nice to meet you, Tanya."

"You too, Swifty," she answers.

Swifty's expression becomes a strange combination of delight mixed with guilt. He seems to feel pretty bad about what happened today.

delight

Tanya climbs into the front seat,

and I jump in the back with Matt and Carly.

While Ronnie and Tanya talk up front, Matt and Carly elbow me in the ribs and mouth "Tanya Billings!" I burst into laughter as we drive back to the set.

One Last Stunt

Part of me thinks it's great that Carly and Matt are here to watch me work. It makes the job seem more real, not like something made up. But another part of me is nervous having two friends watching me do something where falling on my butt is a definite possibility. I don't let my mind wander to the dark area of my brain that says,

resolve

aviator

Matt posted a video of you struggling to read on YouTube. Don't screw up now or he'll do it again. I look at my friends, take a deep breath, and resolve to make them proud.

Collette, the director, puts her arm around Tanya. Her curls, hat, and aviator sunglasses almost hide her face. "Who are your friends?" Collette asks.

Before I can introduce them, Tanya introduces Matt and Carly to Collette. I pray she doesn't ask what they're doing here or where we've been.

"You ready, dude?" Collette asks.

"Ready," I answer.

"The set looks a little different than it did in rehearsals. Check it out."

We follow the director to the

other side of the soundstage, where they've set up a facsimile of a street under construction, complete with bulldozer, flashing lights, caution signs, and actors wearing hard hats.

facsimile

"What do you think?" Collette asks us.

"It looks so real," Carly answers.

"Whoa!" Matt checks out the long row of orange cones set up on the fake street and tries to grab the board out of my hands. "How many are there?"

Collette snaps her gum. "Thirty."

"You have to slalom between thirty cones?" Matt asks me. "Without hitting any—that'll be a first!"

Just as I'm about to scream at Matt, he turns to Collette. "I'm kidding! I've seen Derek do a run of fifty without hitting any," he lies.

When one of the assistants brings Collette something to sign, Matt pulls me aside. "You can do it, Derek. I know you can."

Carly pulls him away from me. "Derek's going to be just fine."

Collette finishes with the assistant and reaches for my board. "May I?"

I hand her my skateboard and follow her to the end of the driveway. "When you get to the end of the run, can you give me a nollie hardflip?" the director asks. "Something like this."

Collette jumps on the board and rides down the driveway. She pops down with her front foot and kicks down with her back. She lets the board rotate as she's in the air, then lands on it with both feet.

The cast and crew applaud and hoot.

"I've been skateboarding since I was your age." She hands me back the board. "Now let's see you."

I tell myself she's asking me to do something I could do in my sleep and will myself to calm down. I jump on my skateboard and give the director my own nollie hardflip, landing a few inches away from her checkerboard sneakers. Tony's behind her, shooting me a giant smile. He's still in his alien costume and holding a parasol to keep cool.

parasol

While Collette talks to one of the cameramen, Matt pulls me aside. "A female director in a Dodgers cap who can skateboard? She's the perfect woman!"

Carly rolls her eyes. "I'm sure she's interested in you too."

When I look over to see if Tanya saw my flip, I find her chatting on her cell, with two assistants hovering around her. But I have more important things to worry about than impressing her: namely, to slalom through thirty cones without falling or knocking any over. I ask Tony what will happen if I do.

"You'll just do it till you get it right. Mistakes are part of the process."

Yet another reason why I wish Tony was our teacher this year.

"We're ready," Collette says. "You two good to go?"

Tony and I tell her we are.

"Hey, you!" she calls to Matt. "I'm the only one shooting here today, got it?"

Matt shyly shuts off his camera and tucks it into his pocket. The assistant with the purple streak in her hair steps in front of me with the clapperboard and says, "Scene 52, take 1."

When Collette yells "action!" I jump on my board and head down the "street" toward the cones with Tony the Alien chasing after me. My mind starts chanting, *Don't mess up, don't mess up, don't mess up, don't mess—* The first cone I hit sends me flying into the street, which doesn't feel so fake upon impact.

impact

"Cut!" Collette runs over to me. "You okay, champ?"

Even though I don't feel like a champ, I tell her I'm fine and watch the prop guys set up the course again.

And again.

And again.

Collette doesn't seem worried and tries to ease the tension with a few jokes. But when the purple-haired assistant is about to yell "Scene 52, take 9," Collette decides we need a five-minute break.

I look up to Matt and Carly, who wave enthusiastically, ignoring the fact that I've blown the last eight takes.

Tony walks over to me with his arms outstretched like a monster. I appreciate his effort, but joking around doesn't dent my stress level.

"Are your friends making you nervous?" Collette asks. "Do you want them to wait for you somewhere else?"

I tell her it's not them; it's me.

"You remember the other day when you let your mind get the best of you, worrying about all the ways you could screw up?" Tony asks.

"It's not my imagination—I *am* messing up!"

He shakes his scaly head. "We *all* have negative thoughts. Overcoming them is what separates pros like us from the rest."

league

Tony's very generous to include me in his league of professionals. "I certainly don't feel like a pro now."

Underneath the green rubber, his eyes are serious. "The big secret is that *nobody* feels like a pro, not even me, and I've been doing this for fifteen years!" He points to his scaly temple. "It's all up here—always has been, always will be. Remember, parkour means getting around obstacles. That's something you'll be doing your whole life, so you might as well get used to it."

Collette raises her hand to hold

off the group of people waiting to ask her questions and tells me to take a few minutes for myself.

Matt runs over, his pockets full of candy bars. "Carly and I are going to go snoop around another part of the set. I've seen you slalom a thousand times. I don't need to watch you again."

"I'm not messing up because you're watching me." I didn't want to tell the others what's bothering me, but I tell Matt. "Suppose I lose Frank because of Swifty? Suppose the woman takes him and I never see him again?"

"That's not going to happen." Matt bites off a giant chunk of chocolate bar. "Dude, you *saved* him today. It was downright heroic. Slaloming down a fake street? Piece of cake!"

Collette approaches and asks if I'm ready to go. Tony comes over too, and Collette shudders when she feels his alien skin.

shudders

"Ready!" I answer.

We head back to our marks as the production assistant says, "Scene 52, take 9."

When Collette calls "action!" I hop on my board and aim for the space between the first two cones. With Tony right behind me, I zigzag through the cones—left, right, left, right—until I get to the end. I kick up my board and do the highest nollie hardflip I've ever done.

I don't think I knocked over any cones but can't turn around to check because the cameras are still rolling, and catching my face on film instead of Tanya's would ruin the take. I wait until Collette says "cut!" before I look back up the hill.

I see only two rows of orange cones perfectly in place.

Collette nods in approval, and the crew applauds. "Pretty nice there, dude. You think you can do it one more time for backup?"

I look up the hill to Matt and Carly, both beaming with pride. I toss back the long hair of my wig and tell Collette I could make that run all day long.

"All I need is one," she says, "but thanks anyway."

As Tony and I walk back up to our marks, I see Tanya waving. I hurry toward her to say good-bye in person, but she's already turned the corner toward her trailer. Easy come, easy go.

As if she can tell what I'm feeling, Carly comes over and tells me I did a great job. I look up to Matt, who gives me a thumbs-up, then I jump on my board to take my final run of the film.

A Short-Lived Victory

deposits

When Ronnie deposits me at home, both Mom and Dad are waiting in the kitchen. Frank's cage is nowhere to be found.

"Where's Frank?" I ask.

"He's next door with one of the interns," Mom answers.

"I was surprised to come home from a meeting to find Jamie in the kitchen with our monkey," Dad says.

"It took a bit of convincing to get him to spill the beans."

My mother's arms are crossed while she waits for my response.

"I wasn't going to hide it from you. I want to tell you everything." I take a seat and update them on the afternoon's events. I even admit it took me nine takes to run the slalom.

My father tells me he's glad I told the truth, but my mother remains silent. When she finally speaks, I hold my breath in anticipation.

"We have to tell the woman from the training organization," she says.

"But for once, it wasn't my fault!" I say. "I don't want to lose Frank because Swifty messed up."

"Breaking into someone's house

and stealing are real offenses," Dad adds. "I'll be calling Swifty's parents tonight."

When I jump out of my chair, Bodi jumps up too. I bend down and comfort him before approaching Mom.

"Do we have to tell the people from the monkey place? Isn't it enough that I got Frank back here safe *and* finished my work in the movie?"

sympathetic

Mom's arms are still crossed, but her eyes look sympathetic. "I think it's best if we're honest with them, don't you?"

"Even if it means losing Frank?" I ask.

"Even if it means losing Frank." She tousles my hair the way she's always done. "Do you want to come to the office? I know a certain monkey who'll be happy to see you."

Before she even finishes the sentence, I'm out the door.

Back to the Old Routine

I sneak into school the next morning, horrified that I might run into Swifty. He and his parents came over last night, and his father made Swifty apologize to my parents, then to me. I've had to say I'm sorry to dozens of parents over the years, but it gave me no pleasure to watch Swifty squirming in his seat.

It might've been my imagination,

squirming

but I thought I saw something in Swifty's eyes that I interpreted as *I'll get you for this*. My mother insisted Swifty's apology was sincere and not to assume the worst. Even so, I'm not taking any chances now— although I feel pretty stupid slinking down the hall behind Ms. Myers and her library cart.

"You still owe me a book, Derek," she whispers to me as I crouch down the hall.

I tell her I'm almost finished— which is an outright lie—then dash into the art room.

I make it through my first two classes by keeping my head down, but when I get out of English, Swifty's waiting by the door.

"Last night was pretty humiliating," he says.

He's almost a head taller than I am, but I gather up enough courage to respond. "You probably should've thought about the consequences before you kidnapped Frank."

ballistic

"My mom went ballistic," Swifty continues. "She took all my video games, and I'm grounded for a month."

I shrug. "Sounds like a reasonable sentence for the crime."

Surprisingly, he agrees with me. "She told me your parents could've called the police. I'm glad they didn't. What I really feel bad about is that you could lose Frank," Swifty says. "I hope they let you keep him."

"Considering it wasn't my fault," I add.

"Considering it wasn't your fault," he repeats.

I leave him standing in the hall alone and head to my next class.

I'm shocked when Ms. McCoddle calls Maria to the front of the room to present her report. These past few weeks have been a blur, and I completely forgot our book reports were due. I look over to Matt and Carly, who both have theirs. The last thing I want to do is have Ms. McCoddle hold me up as an example of a kid who thinks he's got more important things to do than hand in his work. (I *did* have more important things to do but still....)

predicament

Matt notices my predicament and raises his hand when Maria finishes reading. "I don't understand the conflict you talked about in that book. Can you explain that again?"

As soon as Maria answers his

conflict

227 ★

question, Carly raises her hand too. "Have you read any of the author's other books?" Carly asks. "How did this one compare?"

Maria leans against the whiteboard and discusses a few of the author's other books. I look up to see if Ms. McCoddle is suspicious that they're stretching the assignment out, but she nods and asks questions of her own. When Maria sits down, Carly volunteers to go next, and after that Matt does too. Before you know it, the bell rings and class is over.

"You guys are the best," I whisper to Matt and Carly as we gather our things. "I haven't even finished the book yet. You totally bailed me."

"It's the least we can do after you brought us to a movie set," Matt says.

"And let us hang out with Tanya Billings," Carly adds.

As we're leaving the room, Ms. McCoddle calls out to us from her desk. "Just because I taught you three in kindergarten doesn't mean you can pull the wool over my eyes now. I expect you to be fully prepared on Monday, Derek. Got it?"

"Got it."

The three of us hurry down the hall. I'm not worried about how much reading I have to do this weekend or how Ms. McCoddle deciphered our plan. For a minute, I'm not even worried about my meeting with the woman from the monkey organization tonight. All I'm thinking about right now is how great it is to have friends who've got your back when you need it.

deciphered

Yes or No?

The woman from the monkey institute is arriving after dinner, so I plan out how our conversation might go. It's kind of crazy, but doing parkour has helped other parts of my life besides just stunts. I might never see Tony again, but he taught me how important it is to plan and how obstacles can usually be overcome. Who knew you could learn life lessons from a guy who runs down the street on fire?

When the woman arrives, she's not the same grandmother-type who helped Frank settle in with us a few months before. This woman's name is Wendie, and she's harried and grumpy. Thankfully, Frank can't spill the beans about our escapade at the warehouse; he just sits in his clean cage with his full water bottle and looks like the most cared for capuchin in the world.

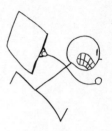

harried

"So," Wendie begins, "can you tell me why poor Frank needed emergency surgery?"

escapade

Before Wendie came, my mother told me I was in charge of this meeting—that she wasn't going to help bail me out this time. When I look over at her now, her arms are

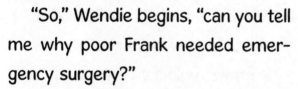

crossed like she has no intention of answering Wendie's question. I explain about the toy horse and how Frank is lucky that my mom is a veterinarian so he had quick medical treatment.

"That's true," Wendie says. "But he would've been better off if he hadn't needed surgery at all, don't you think?"

I look over at Mom who still isn't talking.

"It definitely would've been better if he hadn't swallowed it," I answer. "I know better now."

Wendie unlocks the cage and takes out Frank. She checks Frank's diaper and gives a quick nod of approval when she sees it's clean. Then she talks to him in a baby voice that's even worse than how my mother talks to animals. "And what do you think, Frankie? Do you want to stay with the Fallons or come back to Boston with me?" Her voice gets even more babyish. "Who's Wendie's good boy?"

I look over to Mom for support, but she looks like she's about to burst into laughter. I make a face that says *Don't blow this for me!* so she takes a deep breath and gets serious again.

Wendie turns to me. "Are there any other incidents I should be aware of before I make my decision?"

Mom arches her eyebrow so high, she looks like a cartoon bad guy. I know what she's waiting for, but I still hesitate.

"Well," I begin, "a kid from

hesitate

school—not one of my friends, I want to make that clear—kind of kidnapped Frank this week."

"Excuse me?"

"But you'll be happy to know I got him back home in no time without a scratch."

Wendie holds Frank even closer. "Tell me more."

So I launch into the story of Swifty, emphasizing how quickly I sprang into action to save Frank. "My friends Matt, Carly, Jamie, and Ronnie all helped. Frank has a real support system here." It's a phrase I've heard my mother say a million times, and I hope it impresses Wendie.

She shakes her head. "I'm just not sure this is the right environment for one of our capuchins."

It's the sentence I've been

emphasizing

dreading for weeks, and my entire body slumps with disappointment. When I look up at my mother, her eyebrow is still arched. I know from experience that she's waiting for me to continue. I feel deflated, but Mom's stubborn expression urges me on.

deflated

"It's not my fault," I say. "I can't be held responsible for some lunatic sneaking into our house."

"Did you say lunatic?"

I realize comparing Swifty to a lunatic is not a good choice of words and begin again.

"Our house is so much better for Frank than being in a big room in Boston with lots of other monkeys," I say.

"Actually there's a long list of people waiting to become foster families. He'd be placed with one of them. With a family who takes care of him so he can live to a ripe old age and change the life of a disabled person for the better."

I try my best to be polite but can't let Wendie get away with that last comment.

"I hate to tell you," I say, "but accidents happen all the time, to everyone. Sure, it was stupid for me to leave a toy out for Frank to grab, but that doesn't mean some other family's not going to make mistakes too. Suppose another family on your list cuts a carrot too big and Frank chokes? Suppose he has some kind of seizure and the closest vet is an hour away?"

I point over at my mom, who still hasn't contributed to the

contributed

conversation. "And as far as Swifty goes," I continue, "he really regrets what he did—and not just because his parents punished him." I begin to gather up steam. "Swifty has nothing to do with this discussion anyway."

regrets

"He doesn't?" Wendie asks.

"No, it's about how Frank feels about being part of our family. He *loves* it here. Suppose he gets assigned to a family who doesn't watch old cowboy movies. Frank likes Westerns, did you know that?"

Wendie shakes her head.

"His favorite thing is sitting next to Bodi and me on the couch. He's always so relaxed, with this huge grin on his face."

My words even convince me. Frank *is* the most important part of this discussion. I take a giant risk and hold my arms out toward Frank. Without thinking twice, he leaves the comfort of Wendie's fleshy arms and jumps into mine. He leans his head against my chest and settles in.

"Frank is where he's supposed to be," I finish. "Taking him away now would only confuse him and leave him lonely."

Wendie closes the latch on the cage and doesn't meet my eyes. "So that's your theory? You're some kind of monkey whisperer now? You know how animals think and feel?"

theory

I point across the room. "Maybe it's in my genes. My mom's pretty good with animals too."

Wendie nods and tells my mother she'll be in touch.

For the first time in the meeting, my mother speaks. "My son has presented a good argument," she says. "I hope you consider his points very seriously."

Wendie grabs her purse from the kitchen table. "I'll give you a call tomorrow with my decision."

After Wendie leaves, my mother holds out her arms for Frank. I guess she needs some comfort after all this tension too.

persuasive

"You were very persuasive," she admits. "But it's out of our hands."

My body finally collapses with the stress and fear of losing my monkey, and I slide onto the closest chair. When Frank tilts his head away from my mom and looks at me, it's almost as if he's asking, *Are you okay?*

I'll let you know tomorrow.

Rut-Ro

lopsided

When I walk into the kitchen the next morning, my father's wearing this lopsided smile while he talks on the phone. The guy is just too weird.

I grab a cookie and head to the door, but he stops me. "He's right here." The grin on his face is even sillier when he hands me the phone.

"Is it Wendie?" I whisper. "Can we keep Frank?"

"It's not Wendie," he answers.

"Then who is it?"

His only answer is that ludicrous expression. I put the phone to my ear.

ludicrous

"Hi, Derek. It's Tanya Billings. How are you?"

As I stare at the phone, my father shrugs as if to say *I told you.* I finally get it together and tell Tanya I'm fine.

"Did you see the video on You-Tube?" she asks.

Please don't say someone got their hands on Matt's video of me reading! I tell her I haven't and race to Dad's laptop in the next room.

"At first I was angry," she admits. "But it's been great! It's gotten more than two hundred thousand hits."

"Uhm, what's the video called?" I'm almost afraid to know.

"Tanya Billings saves wild monkey."

"What?" Sure enough, a video comes up of Tanya climbing a wall of crates to save a capuchin monkey. The video stops short just as she reaches the top of the shelving.

Except it isn't Tanya. It's me.

"My phone hasn't stopped ringing," she says. "People think I do my own stunts now. Did you tell your friend to post this? You're a genius!"

As I watch myself climb up to Frank for the second time, I try and decide if I should tell Tanya that I had nothing to do with Matt posting this video, but I keep quiet. I'm just glad Frank is high up enough that you can't really see it's him. Wendie doesn't seem like the YouTube type, but you never know. Today is the day I find out if we keep him, and I don't want anything to mess it up.

"First using illustrations to help me with my lines, then giving me this great free publicity—I'm so glad I met you."

publicity

Before I can ask her what movie she's working on next or if she wants to come over sometime, she hangs up. I stare into the silent phone and know in my heart it's the last time I'll ever talk to Tanya Billings.

I text Matt.

r u insane? y did you post it?

He answers me back moments later.

Cuz u climb like a girl.

But he apologizes for posting the video without my permission and says he'll take it down if I want him to. I tell him to keep it up.

My father hands me a carrot dipped in peanut butter. "Isn't Ronnie coming?"

"I think he's had enough of me for one week," I answer. "He's scheduled for next Tuesday instead."

"So you're finishing the book on your own?"

"I *am* twelve," I respond. "Reading without help *is* a possibility."

My mother comes in from her office and passes over an envelope addressed to me. I can't remember the last time I got any real mail. I'm even more aghast by what's inside.

aghast

"Is this a joke?" I ask.

Dad looks over my shoulder at the check from the studio and whistles. "That's more than all the birthday money you've ever gotten in your life."

"Multiplied by ten," Mom adds.

"Don't tell the studio," I whisper. "But I would've worked on that movie for free."

"You should add that to your college fund," Dad suggests.

I'll have to get Mom to take me to the promenade in Santa Monica to blow some of this money before they have any other bright ideas.

I spend the next several hours reading my book and drawing my vocabulary words. But what I mostly do is look at the clock. Before I can even ask the question, my mother answers.

"She'll call soon," Mom says.

"She's doing this to torture me, I just know it."

"Believe it or not, Derek, it's not always about you." She balances a stack of towels on her hip and heads upstairs.

I check my email and am surprised to see one with an attachment. It's a quick note from Tony.

Thought you'd like to see this.
It was great working with you.
I'll keep you in mind next time
I need a Super Stuntboy.

I open the attached file. It's a photograph the set photographer took last week. Tony and I are at the very top of the junkyard pile, planning our way around dozens of obstacles. Even though this is a photograph and not a video, I can hear Tony's words as if we were standing up there now. *You can do this. Take it slow and plan it out.*

I suppose it's good advice for any project, and it gives me the energy to concentrate for another hour on my work. When the phone rings, I bound across the room and stand beside my father.

"Yes," he says into the phone. "I understand completely."

My mother seems as anxious about hearing Wendie's decision as I am. My father talks for a few more moments before hanging up and turning to us.

"We can keep him," he says.

I jump into the air, but my father's stern expression sends me crashing back down to earth.

probation

"But only on probation," he continues. "They want to talk to us once a week, have us fill out a monthly report, and they'll revisit the decision in ninety days."

Mom nods her head. "That's fair."

"It's *not* fair," I say. "They're never going to find another family who loves Frank as much as we do."

outweighed

"They have a long wait list," Dad continues. "But they felt Mom having a veterinary practice right next door outweighed the risks."

"You mean the risk of having a classmate kidnap Frank again? Or the risk of me leaving out a toy?"

adolescent

"Believe it or not, they didn't blame you for Swifty. They were more concerned about Frank's safety in the home with an adolescent."

I'm not sure, but I think that means me.

"You have a real opportunity to prove yourself here," Mom tells me. "You're lucky to have a second chance."

Three months of waiting to find out if I can hang out with Frank for a few more years hardly seems lucky to me, but it's definitely better than having Wendie pull up to the house today and take him away forever.

Mom removes Frank from his cage. Instead of cuddling him, she holds him with outstretched arms.

"He's all yours," she says as she hands him to me.

My mother's one of the smartest people around. I was so worried about losing Frank that she knows the last thing I'd do now is whine about Frank's daily maintenance. The strange thing is, I don't mind doing it; I *want* to take care of Frank, even if it means dealing with rubber gloves and monkey poop.

"Okay, big guy," I say. "You're coming with me."

cunning

As I walk to Mom's office with Frank in my arms, I swear he gives me a cunning little wink. Which makes me wonder who's training who around here.

Same Old, Same Old

Ms. McCoddle wastes no time calling on me first thing Monday morning, as if she spent her weekend planning for this very moment.

"My book is the second one in a series," I begin. "The first was more of a mystery, but this one focuses on a boy and his best friend."

"Go on," Ms. McCoddle says.

As I scan the words I've written,

I get a sudden jolt that reminds me of the YouTube video Matt posted. The memory is physical, like a stab in the gut.

"Are you all right, Derek?" Ms. McCoddle asks.

cubicle

I don't want to tell her that every time I read out loud, I still worry that I'll mess up or that I'll be a bad reader my entire life or that I'll be a grown man working in a cubicle, still drawing pictures of vocabulary words.

Instead, I inform Ms. McCoddle that I'm fine and inch my way through the next paragraph. I look up at the end of a sentence to glance at Matt, whose eager expression urges me on.

"There was lots of adventure in this book, lots of jumping and running, which I liked. There were also moments that were pretty moving, even upsetting. I got through those parts as fast as possible so I could return to the sections with action."

Tom raises his hand and asks about one of the animals in the book. I answer in so much detail that Ms. McCoddle finally cuts me off.

"Is that all?" she asks.

"Isn't that enough? I mean, I read a whole book!" I head back to my seat.

As the others give their reports, I open up my sketchbook to the photo of Bodi and Frank I took this week-end. They're sitting next to each other on the couch, and you can see my reflection in the mirror behind them as I take their picture. Ninety days of paperwork and phone calls seem like a modern-day torture device, but if that's what's required to keep Frank, that's what I'll do.

The rest of the day goes by incredibly slowly, the way some movie scenes use slow motion to emphasize something cool like a car driving off a cliff.

Later, in Ms. Decker's class, I stare out the window and imagine the premiere of Collette's film with Tanya Billings and me getting out of a limousine in front of the Mann Village Theatre. Tanya wears a sparkly gold dress, and I'm in a tuxedo—maybe even with a beret and a silver walking stick. We eat lots of free popcorn during the movie, and the audience gasps when I perform my death-defying stunts. Afterward we

limousine

go to a party with giant ice sculptures and a make-your-own-sundae bar while hundreds of people clamor for our autographs.

clamor

A series of coughs brings me back to reality. Carly's across the aisle, and when I look over at her, she scribbles on a piece of paper, then holds it up. *Stop grinning!*

I wave her off and try to focus on Ms. Decker in the front of the classroom. I know my daydream is completely ridiculous—I won't be invited to the premiere, and hardly anyone will know I'm in the film— but still the whole adventure was positive. It makes me wonder what other great surprises are in store for me this year. The possibilities are endless, and I want to race out of the classroom to explore them all.

But reality crashes in when I see Ms. Decker standing beside me.

"Derek? What do you think?" she asks.

I look over to Carly, then Matt, who both seem pretty amused that Ms. Decker nabbed me while I was daydreaming.

"Uhm . . . a monkey?"

vaccine

Several kids laugh, and Ms. Decker shakes her head. "No, I'm afraid the person who invented the polio vaccine was *not* a monkey. Maria?"

I shrug and let someone else scramble for an answer.

Which is fine, because my limo awaits.

About the Author

Janet Tashjian is the author of many popular novels, including *My Life as a Book*; the Larry series—*The Gospel According to Larry*, *Vote for Larry*, and *Larry and the Meaning of Life*—as well as *Fault Line*; *Multiple Choice*; *Tru Confessions*; and *Marty Frye, Private Eye*. She lives with her family in Los Angeles, California. www.janettashjian.com

author

About the Illustrator

Jake Tashjian is the illustrator of *My Life as a Book*. He has been drawing pictures of his vocabulary words on index cards since he was a kid and now has a stack taller than a house. When he's not drawing, he loves to surf, read comic books, and watch movies.

illustrator